Trailing
the
Schoolchildren's
Blizzard

Trailing
the
Schoolchildren's
Blizzard

B. Lois Thieszen Preheim

RESOURCE *Publications* · Eugene, Oregon

TRAILING THE SCHOOLCHILDREN'S BLIZZARD

Wipf & Stock
An Imprint of Wipf and Stock Publishers
199 W. 8th Ave., Suite 3
Eugene, OR 97401

www.wipfandstock.com

PAPERBACK ISBN: 978-1-6667-0325-2
HARDCOVER ISBN: 978-1-6667-0326-9
EBOOK ISBN: 978-1-6667-0327-6

Manufactured in the U.S.A.

Dedication

This book is dedicated to all who
look back in order to see the future,
who recognize what has been and what is,
and who figure out what can be.

Tracking The Schoolchildren's Blizzard
JANUARY 1888

JANUARY 11
Eddie
FROM
Edmonton

JANUARY 11
June
FROM
Saskatoon

JANUARY 12
Mark
FROM
Bismarck

JANUARY 12
Paul
FROM
St. Paul

JANUARY 11
Helen
FROM
Helena

JANUARY 12
Maria
FROM
Freeman

JANUARY 12
Katharina and Lena
FROM
Henderson

JANUARY 12
Gertrune
FROM
Newton

JANUARY 12
Edith
FROM
Enid

JANUARY 14
Austin
FROM
Austin

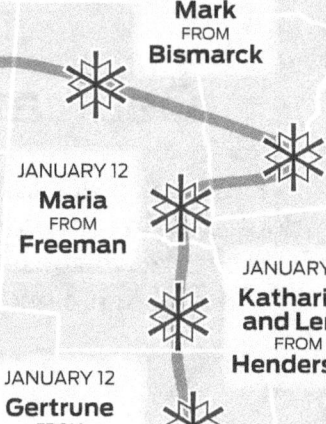

Contents

Prologue

Why should the January 12, 1888 blizzard be remembered more than other storms that have had more snow, stronger winds, and colder temperatures? When snow, sudden strong winds, and colder temperatures strike so quickly and without warning, this storm becomes particularly memorable. This storm is also remembered because most people were caught off guard; unseasonably warm temperatures preceded the suddenness of the blizzard.

The words "suddenly" and "struck without warning" are often used to describe why many were unprepared for the instant change in weather. Unpreparedness, including insufficient fuel at the schoolhouse, led to tragedy for many schoolteachers and schoolchildren. Guidelines frequently follow a laissez-faire procedure that is found wanting. Within a few weeks following the blizzard, the Nebraska State Superintendent sent a letter to rural schools instructing them to have winter fuel on the school premises and under roof before cold weather sets in. This significantly changed how rural schools prepared for winter in the years that followed.

This storm affected the Great Plains population, regardless of age, social status, profession, economic level, or level of intelligence. The stories of people caught in the January 12, 1888 blizzard reveal a variety of ways they used resources creatively. These men, women, and children discovered ingenious ways to protect themselves. Ingenuity met the challenge of survival.

While one admires the fortitude of the blizzard survivors, we also must sympathize with those suffering anguish and death that day and the days following.

❄   ❄   ❄

Temperatures in the narrative are given in Fahrenheit unless otherwise indicated.

Preface

I am fascinated with oral and written stories of the January 12, 1888 blizzard because people I know remembered hearing these stories and then retold them, relating the impact of that day. My late mother-in-law, Sieglinda Waltner Preheim, of Freeman, South Dakota, grew up within one-fourth of a mile from where the five frozen boys (whom I write about in Chapter Six) were found. Growing up in Henderson, Nebraska, I was aware of a blizzard survival story in that community, detailed in Chapter Seven. To share a bigger picture of this storm, my goal was to link people with family stories of the blizzard to those in other places who were also keepers of blizzard stories.

I wondered about other blizzard stories along the storm's path.

As I travel in retirement with my husband, Ron, we frequent museums to immerse ourselves in the culture of a location. On occasion, I spend time in university or city archives, while my husband reads or visits factories and agriculture-related places. My interest in the Great Blizzard grew from only wondering about the impact of the blizzard in different locations to collecting stories and newspaper clippings. Following the trail of this blizzard expanded when I received the Saskatchewan Archives Board Research Pass. I spent many happy hours combing through newspapers and reading books of the 1888 era and becoming familiar with the landscape and history of selected places.

My tote filled rapidly with collected data. I faced the choice of either doing something with my material or chucking the contents of my collection. If I wrote a book, would I have something to say that hadn't already been said? It occurred to me that by following the blizzard trail with stories of families encountering the blizzard, I could document the larger picture of the storm's path in an interesting way. I then mapped out towns and cities along the storm's route. The cities and towns were self-selected since they were the places from where I had information. However, that information was usually from a male perspective, adding another layer of urgency. I wanted to hear how a female, whether child or adult, would express herself while living through the impact of the storm. I wondered if the female voice could be integrated into these stories in a balanced way.

I decided now was the ideal time to do that.

To give validity to my research, I needed to find weather maps from selected cities and towns or of those in close proximity. I relied heavily on the National Archives of the United States Weather Bureau Climatological Records for 1819-1892 and the Government of Canada Historical Climate Data link (https://climate.weather.gc.ca/historical_data/search_historic_data_e.html). They became the backbone of the blizzard trail, supplying me with data from historical weather records and the structure from which to proceed. I was surprised to discover that the plunge in cold temperatures consistently came three days after the onslaught of the sudden storm – the storm that caught so many people off guard in a huge region of North America. In some cases, the low temperature for that day still holds the all-time record.

Writing this book has taken me on a journey through the Great Plains. On the wall near my computer hangs a framed world map. It is a gift from our children and their families with a sentiment I treasure. Written on the map, in cursive with a black wide-tipped marker, are these words: "It's not where you go, but who sits beside you on the journey." I invite you to make yourself comfortable as you sit beside me and travel through the pages of time to the second week of January 1888.

Introduction

The January 12, 1888 blizzard is well-known and has been the subject of books and newspaper articles. But many stories have not yet been widely shared. In some cases, we have a written history; in others, oral history. Sometimes there are lots of details and other times very few. I've taken the liberty of blending what we know with what we can imagine. Thus, consider this book historical fiction – rooted in truth with observations and speculation to help tell these rich stories more deeply and fully.

I hope to expand the scope of our common perception of the 1888 blizzard as an isolated storm to that of a massive, connected blizzard trail that includes tragic and heroic events. Many accounts of this storm overlook the broader impact of this well-remembered day.

During the second week of January 1888, a massive invasion of Arctic air from the North-West Territories plunged into southwestern Canada, birthing a blizzard that stormed through the center of the United States. Its tempestuous energy brought snow, wind, and frigid cold blasting from Canada through Montana, Dakota Territory, Minnesota, Nebraska, Kansas, Oklahoma, Texas, and beyond. Because the storm struck on a school day, children going to school, at school, or returning home were among those who took the biggest brunt of its suddenness and severity. That has led many to refer to this storm as the "schoolchildren's blizzard."

Each chapter features a different family in the storm's path. A recurring theme of these stories is how parents, children, teachers, and community people work together as they either submit to or conquer nature's elements. Holding the chapters together is the common thread of experiencing the storm's fury. Each chapter begins with a poem encapsulating the family events and ends with a recipe to help the reader experience, in a personal way, the elements of a place and time.

People of all ages will identify with varying facets of decision-making. By pulling together stories of ingenuity, observation, intuition, and problem-solving during this historic 1888 blizzard, I want to remind readers of the tenacity that pioneers demonstrated as they coexisted with nature's fury. Hopefully, it will spark and nurture creativity as readers respond to new and unexpected situations in their future.

My perspective is influenced by farm life, education, and being female. Living on a crop and livestock farm most of my life in the midwestern United States, I know firsthand how awareness of weather determines decisions. As an educator involved in both teaching and administration, I value integrating knowledge with application. As a woman, I am conscious of how our voices are heard and interpreted. That's why I've included stories about and from women's point of view, voices that have been frequently overlooked.

This year (2020), the United States is celebrating one hundred years of women's right to vote. The Nineteenth Amendment to the United States Constitution, ratified August 18, 1920, gave women a voice at the polls. My hope is that this book will give pioneer women who lived during the January 12, 1888 blizzard a voice, and that we gain new awareness and acknowledge the significance of women's voices in our history.

I hope these stories help redeem their voices from the past and send sound waves reverberating into the future.

B. Lois Thieszen Preheim – August 2020

Eddie

My name is Eddie
and I am nearly thirteen.
It is the eleventh of January eighteen eighty-eight.
Snow comes in a cascade of floating flakes.
The temperature plummets,
deepening the cellar of cold.
Wind from the north whines and whirrs.
We live on an animal farm
growing grains and fodder.
I want to know what makes cold cold.
My mother, Wintaka, tells me
on our earth, temperature, and
air pressure seek a balance;
I am trying to understand.
The glacier of cold is moving south,
invading the unsuspecting.
Observation and prediction –
that interests me.

CHAPTER ONE

Eddie from Edmonton

Located in the District of Alberta (al BER ta) in Canada

Date: January 11, 1888
High: 12 F. (-11.7 C.)
Low: -28 F. (-32 C.)
Wind: N

E ddie Lehman, almost a teenager – he will turn thirteen in the fall – shivers, even with a bearskin draped over his shoulders.

"Mom, tell me why it is so cold this winter!"

Not quite sure what Eddie is really asking, Wintaka lapses into one of the tales about the cold that she learned from her mother. But the story of the bear using his tail for ice fishing, ending with a curtailed stump of a tail, doesn't quite cut it for Eddie.

"I'm not a kid anymore, Mom," he protests. "I want to know what makes our weather colder than usual this January."

Wintaka, a former school teacher, is very aware of her surroundings

1

and is delighted to observe and satisfy Eddie's quest for knowledge. She loves describing what she sees and hears, and what makes sense to her imaginative mind. Teaching is her passion and was her life before meeting Edward Lehman, a farmer who moved to Alberta from the East. He was looking for land to grow barley and oats, and raise farm animals like ducks, geese, chickens, pigs, cows, and horses. Edward, in the 1870s, equated moving west with opportunity for farming in Alberta, located in the North-West Territories of Canada.

Edward and Wintaka met at Edmonton's Town Center, a gathering place for locals wanting to socialize and purchase needed items. And it's a place for those new in town to learn more about available resources. Edward was full of questions. Wintaka, rather intrigued with this new fellow in town, made herself available as his local tour guide. They became good friends, and soon very good friends.

Winnie, as Edward affectionately calls her, is the daughter of a fur-trapping family living near the northern forests. Trapping for beaver, muskrat, and mink, and trading them for necessities, is a "close to nature" way of life for her family. Attending a mission school as a youth, Wintaka soaked up everything from learning about life in permanent homes to learning about an orderly way of life and the order of the universe. As a star pupil, she helped the teachers as needed, but returned to her family whenever possible. Teaching a few months during the year at the local mission supplemented their income and she enjoyed it. She also enjoyed learning from her dad, Geo Dupray, a Frenchman who explored much of the area. He loves maps and studies the surveys done by earlier fur traders.

Wintaka's mom, Lila Star, is from the Blackfeet people. She has always wondered what the future holds for their daughter, a *Metis*, someone of mixed racial parenthood.

Wintaka's family was fortunate in settling on this plot of ground because of the proximity to a stream for fishing and trapping and the forest for wood and hunting. Three years ago, there was a rebellion against the Canadian government by the *Metis* people (mostly children of a French parent who had married someone of First Nations descent). The *Metis* wanted assurance they could own land and have a voice in government. The future of Geo Dupray and Lila Star's land title was of concern. Would they be able to pass on this plot of land to Wintaka one day? They were relieved when the government agreed that the *Metis* could own land and have government representation. However, the native people who stayed within their tribe were strongly encouraged to move elsewhere. The government wanted to open the lands to white pioneers for settlement.

The North-West Mounted Police was organized in 1874 to stop illegal liquor trade between the First Nations of Canada and people from Montana. Introducing alcohol brought addiction, dependence, and hunger to First Nations people. The government's forced removal of many of these indigenous families from their homes to reservations opened this vast area of land for settlers to claim.

Life changed for Wintaka when she married Edward. She feared she could no longer teach. Edward expected a wife to devote her time to home and family. But this agrarian patriarchal mindset didn't seem right to her. With a healthy dose of self-respect, early in their marriage Wintaka asked Edward about his views.

"Edward, you are very good at being a farmer. I am very good at being a teacher. Why would you expect me to give up what I am good at and enjoy doing?"

"Now, Wintaka, suppose we have a family. Who will take care of the little one and who will cook for me?" countered Edward.

"It seems to me you haven't exactly starved by cooking for yourself," she teased. "So we know that isn't the real issue. Caring for the little one is another matter. What if your mother-in-law were to help look after our child for a few days a week? Would that make a difference?"

"Wintaka, it takes courage for me to think differently about what I have been taught – or should I say have observed," Edward said. "I see your point, but I need to think about it and get used to the idea."

"It took courage for me to bring up my view too, Edward. Thank you for considering my feelings about my profession."

It took time, but eventually Edward agreed that Wintaka could be available to help teach as needed, as she had been doing. "I'll even help with the little one, providing it isn't planting or harvest season, of course," Edward said with a wink. Edward's attempt at humor gave him space to adjust to a different way of thinking.

Wintaka and Edward wanted a family and agreed that if their newborn was a boy, he will be called Eddie, short for Edward, and if a girl, she will be called Winnie after Wintaka. In the fall of 1875, Eddie was born.

Eddie, an only child, loves being entertained by his mom with stories of nature, animals, and weather, especially when school isn't in session. The non-missionary schools in 1888 have a "hit and miss" schedule, usually decided by the teacher, although four years ago, the federal government decreed that children ages seven through twelve should attend school for twelve weeks a year. This is Eddie's last year of school, with his thirteenth birthday coming this fall.

Wintaka's arms encircle Eddie's slight frame as she wraps the bearskin around her son in the cold January air this Wednesday morning.

"Fair enough, Eddie, there are some things you already know about where you live. Remember the miniature earth we made several years ago; how we took the stomach of the bear and packed it with soft snow and then let it freeze outside? We then wrapped it with strips of softened soaked bark dipped in a mixture of pasty flour and water."

Eddie holds his tummy and chuckles as he remembers.

"I could hardly wait for the roundish shaped earth to dry so we could punch a small hole in the stomach for the melting snow to drain. Drawing a line around the belly of the earth by mixing soot and liquid to mark the equator is a happy memory. How messy, but fun!"

The once-upon-a-time teacher smiles and reflects on the project.

"The latitude markings of repeated ten degrees were drawn on both sides of the equator. Every degree represents 115 kilometers or about sixty-nine miles. Now Eddie, the city of Edmonton is considered the Gateway to the North. You have heard us talk about the cold coming from north of the 60th parallel, which is in the North-West Territories. People living there get even fewer sun hours than we do."

Eddie interjects, excitedly recalling the winter solstice just three weeks ago. "I remember that the shortest day of the year for light is the winter solstice, with only six hours of daylight. It takes a lot of candles and fuel for the lantern with so much darkness!"

Wintaka places a lit candle in Eddie's hand to represent the sun. She wants to make sure Eddie understands that not only are there limited hours of sunlight, but the tilting away from the sun reduces the intensity of its light. With the model of the earth in her hands, Wintaka walks around the "sun," the candle held by her son, tilting the "earth" to demonstrate her point.

"See how little light reaches the spot where our home is located? We get very little warmth from the sun these days. And then, because of the way our spot on the earth tilts away from the sun, the cold earth doesn't really warm up. The cold air from the North-West Territories keeps the ground even colder."

Eddie's eyes light up.

"There is one thing I know about warm air – it rises. Before we go to bed, you and Dad fix a big warm fire. My bed in the loft is close to the ceiling – I can feel the warmth."

Wintaka is thrilled that Eddie understands this.

"You are right! The warm air from the fire likes to go up. We scurry around getting ready for bedtime, stirring the cold air close to our feet as we move about. Cold air outside stays close to the ground, and the layer of cold gets thicker unless winds stir the cold and there is enough warm air around to rise."

Eddie quickly nods his head, reviewing what he heard his mother explain; he gets it.

"So this January is cold to begin with because of the angle of the earth away from the sun, and there isn't enough warm air rising, so it just gets colder and colder. And the layer of cold gets deeper and deeper. Where, then, can added warmth come from?" he asks.

Wintaka introduces Eddie to two other players in the making of their weather.

"The Rocky Mountains and the Pacific Ocean to the west affect the temperatures too," she explains.

"You may think the warmer and more moist air from the ocean will rise and slide east of the mountains. But sometimes the moist, warm air doesn't have enough momentum to get over the mountain range because of the unseen blanket of cold pressing down. This pressing or pushing down of the warm windy air so that it can't get over the mountains is called high pressure."

Eddie scratches his head.

"So then the opposite of high pressure, a cold blanket pressing down, is low pressure, with the warm moist air rising?"

"Exactly," she says, and then makes a comparison using Eddie's observation.

"The big factors are sunlight and stirring breezes. It's just like at bedtime – there is warmth from the fire and your dad and I are shuffling around. This stirs the warm air and that helps it rise. Let's be thankful for sunlight and a breeze. Remember, the earth is in constant search of balance, whether it is temperature or air pressure."

With a twinkle in her eye, Wintaka mentions lunch and recipes.

"It is almost lunchtime, and I plan to use Grandma Lila's recipe to make your favorite berry drink to go with our bear patties. But before we start lunch, I'll give you some weather-related recipes. All of this will help answer your grown-up question of why it is so cold."

Eddie feels more like an adult than a child as he talks with his mom about the making of cold weather, which is raging outside. Roads are all blocked and nothing is moving.

In the meantime, unbeknownst to the Lehman family, the cold air on the ground is expanding into a huge mass of cold air – an imaginary glacier – moving southward. There are some hours of reprieve from the extreme cold as the mercury rises. It begins to snow, a slow, never-ending cascade of huge flakes. Before the night is over, snow accumulates to five inches. Wind increases, swirling the snow around.

WEATHER-RELATED 'RECIPES'

COLD WEATHER

INGREDIENTS
  Sunlight
  Cold air

METHOD
  Sprinkle a pinch of sunlight to heat the ground, about five to six
    hours.
  Block mild and moist air from the Pacific Ocean (and other bodies
    of water).
  Wait a week; it will get colder and enlarge the area of cold ground
    – think about a moving glacier of air.

ADD
  Clear sky

RESULT
  Guaranteed colder temperature by morning – clouds serve as
    an insulating blanket and keep temperatures from dropping
    overnight.

OPTION
  Clean white snow – sunlight on snow is reflected back into the
    atmosphere before the earth can absorb warmth so it will
    remain cold.

HIGH PRESSURE

INGREDIENTS
Arctic air (heavy, cold)
Sunlight

METHOD
Press down cold Arctic air (pressure) over moist, warm air that
wants to rise.
Wait for wind.

ADD
Wind – stir into a pocket of warm, moist air.

RESULT
Nature is looking for a way of connecting the variables of
temperature, pressure, and wind. Keep in mind that the rotation
of a planet that has oceans, irregular landmasses, and mountains
adds to the variables that may affect the airflow.

LOW PRESSURE

INGREDIENTS
Air that is moist and humid
Sunlight

METHOD
Let sunshine warm accumulated water.
Moisture rises, forming clouds high in the sky.
Warm moist air is pulled up.

RESULT
High cold air pushes the warm moist air down. Cold air aloft
actually increases the lift. The air becomes saturated as it ascends
and rain/snow falls.
Rain or snow, depending on the temperature, pours out of the
clouds.

RECIPE
BERRY MILK DRINK
Drink from a hollow quill (straw).

UTENSILS
   Cup or drinking glass
   Quill from a goose wing

INGREDIENTS
   Whey (the liquid left from making butter) or milk mixed with
      chocolate or berry juice to taste
   Honey to taste

METHOD
   Pour favorite drink such as whey or flavored milk in a cup or
      drinking glass with honey.
   Stir.
   Place quill in liquid and put lips over the top portion of the hollow
      quill.
   Inhale, keeping lips firmly on the quill.

RESULT
   Air is removed from the inside of the straw. This creates a vacuum,
      thus letting the pressure of air outside the straw push the liquid
      upward into your mouth.

June

My name is June
and I am fifteen.
It is the eleventh of January eighteen eighty-eight.
The icy cold and wintry fingers
find my little sister and me.
It is an Arctic hurricane
and a minus thirty-five degree Fahrenheit
with a windchill again as much.
Our comfortable log cabin is home.
We wrap ourselves in blankets,
telling stories of berries, bears,
and a friend with a clay pot.
Our parents tend the store,
the front part of our cabin.
We live close to trails of rail.
New settlers come and supplies arrive.
I wonder what my friend's name is,
the one with a clay pot.

CHAPTER TWO

June from Saskatoon

Located in the District of Saskatchewan (sass CATCH uh wahn) in Canada

Date: January 11, 1888
High: 23 F. (-5 C.)
Low: -35 F. (-38 C.)
Wind: NW

It's been very cold in southern Saskatchewan. Today is Wednesday, and snow has fallen since mid-morning. As evening approaches, the wind increases. Low temperatures in January average 20 to 10 degrees below zero, but this evening it is like an Arctic hurricane with 35 degrees below zero. The wind makes it feel even colder.

June, who is fifteen, lives with her family in the back room of a store on the southern edge of Saskatoon. She dislikes the frigid weather; she much prefers the gentle summer winds that roll across the open prairie. Her mother, Malinda Bergen, sells coffee, tea, and baked treats in their store. Her father, Donald Bergen, keeps supplies on hand for

11

travelers and settlers. June often is expected to entertain her six-year-old sister, Sally.

The Canadian Pacific Railway came through Saskatchewan five years ago and brought settlers to the area and supplied the store with building materials. Saskatoon was a relatively new town founded by John N. Lake in 1882, a year before the railroad was completed.

Enticed with the idea and possibility of starting a business, June and Sally's parents decided four years ago to move to the western frontier, traveling by railway. The competitive nature of supply and demand in Toronto from the growing number of merchants prompted the Bergen family to look elsewhere for business opportunities. They knew that where there is a railroad, settlers will come. Wherever there are settlers, goods, seeds, and equipment will be needed. Deliveries by rail make specific orders a convenient method of supplying needs. The girls hope their grandparents, both Mama's and Papa's parents, will come from the East soon to the wide-open spaces of the prairies. Grandpa Bergen teases the children that it must be really windy, as there is "air" in "prairie," where they now live.

Saskatoon is in the District of Saskatchewan. Six years ago, the Canadian government designated four districts between Manitoba and British Columbia: Alberta, Saskatchewan, Assiniboia (uh SIN ih BOY uh), and Athabaska (a tha BAS ka). South of Saskatoon is the 90,000-square-mile District of Assiniboia, named after a settlement of Native Americans. Some natives live in teepees near the sheltered areas not far from the river. Others left for Montana or a reservation.

While politics and government policies change over the years, the cycle of weather remains a constant. Faced with the blast of bitter cold on this January day, the Bergen sisters concoct a creative way to travel to a warmer place and time.

"Tell me the story about when you picked Saskatoon berries," begs Sally as she climbs onto June's lap. They wrap a blanket around themselves, hoping to keep each other warm. Sally, with a big "please" and a smile, snuggles under the blanket with her big sister and the storytelling begins to transport them from a bitter cold January evening to a mild July afternoon.

June begins. "'It's a good day to pick Saskatoon berries, June, but be careful of bears,' Mama warns as she hands me the berry basket."

"The weather is lovely, and carrying my reed berry basket with a handle, I can swing the basket as I skip and hum a tune at the same time. As I am nearing a ravine not too far from the Saskatchewan River, I find bushes twice my size that are big and round. Saskatoon berries are small and purple. I can bend the branches and reach the berries up high. I am as happy as I can be. Mama will make the berries into pie, cobbler, *plautz* (berries and sugar, mixed with a bit of cornstarch for thickening, on stretched dough), or muffins. Or she will dry them to use for winter baking. I start picking berries and I am amazed how fast my basket fills up."

"Suddenly, I notice on the opposite side of the bush that branches are moving. My heart beats faster and I stop picking berries. Could it be a bear? What should I do! I don't move. Again there is movement on the other side of the bush. I hold my breath; could it be a – a – a – ? Then I see a hand reach for a cluster of berries. I put my free hand over my mouth. With my other hand, I clutch my basket handle tightly. I remove my hand from my mouth and push aside some branches and look. Our eyes meet."

"And what do you see?" Sally asks, though she already knows what happens next. She claps her hands gleefully and finishes the story.

"There is a girl with a clay pot gathering berries. You both smile, then show each other your Saskatoon berries, and then you run all the way home and tell us about how you met your new friend."

The story is over, but the wind continues to howl and the snow continues to fly as the Bergen family prepares for bedtime in their comfortable log cabin home.

Those who are out in the elements on the evening of January 11 soon change their plans when the sudden wind swirls the blinding snow. Many people report an unplanned search for shelter where host and guest alike make a night of it. This is a night of surprises and hospitality. By morning, life is back to normal even though it is cold. But the wind continues blowing southeast to Montana and beyond.

❋   ❋   ❋

The next day, an article in a Saskatchewan newspaper reports that a Mr. Mears near Saskatoon had gone to the barn not far from his house to do chores and had gotten lost. Tracks indicated that he had wandered in a southeasterly direction, the direction of the blowing wind.

❋   ❋   ❋

In Saskatoon, it is said there is no such thing as bad weather, only a bad choice of what to wear.

❄ ❄ ❄

RECIPE
SASKATOON BERRY MUFFINS

Bake at 400° for 25 minutes.
Yields 12-15 muffins

UTENSILS
   Bowl, medium size, for dry ingredients
   Bowl, small size, for milk, egg, and melted butter
   Cup, for berries
   Spoon to stir
   Muffin tin

INGREDIENTS
   Flour 2 cups
   Baking powder 4 t.
   Salt 1/2 t.
   Sugar 6 T.
   Butter 3 T. melted
   Egg 1
   Milk 1 cup
   Saskatoon berries or berries of choice 1 cup

OPTIONAL
   Berries 1/2 cup dried instead of fresh berries

METHOD
   Measure flour, and reserve 3 T. to dust fresh berries.
   Add the baking powder, salt, and sugar to rest of flour.
   Mix dry ingredients and set aside.
   Mix beaten egg, melted butter, and milk.
   Combine with dry ingredients, stirring about 10 times.
   Fold in berries, stirring 3 more times.
   Fill greased muffin tin 2/3 full.

Helen

My name is Helen
and I am already fourteen.
It is the eleventh of January eighteen eighty-eight.
By evening the below-zero cold
creeps through clothes and skin.
The fifty-mile-an-hour wind
blows snow horizontally
with boomerang speed.
Our family owns a ranch,
a cattle ranch with fences.
Swirling snow and strong wind confuse animals.
Cattle drift with wind to a ravine
trampling the first to stumble
only to freeze atop the heap.
Dad and my brother, Dennis, look for strays.
A wagon on sled-like runners
awaits its mission. I put hay inside the wagon.
Mom fortifies family with sausage,
pancakes, and Canadian syrup.
Surviving cattle must be found and fed.

CHAPTER THREE

Helen from Helena

Located in Montana Territory
of the United States of America

January 11, 1888
High: 38.5 F. (3 C.)
Low: 18.5 F. (-10 C.)
Wind: SW

Grabbing the covers in her sleep, Helen Harding, fourteen, wakes up with a start. There is activity stirring downstairs in the kitchen near the partition with the potbelly stove. Bounding down the stairs with clothes in hand, she greets everyone.

"Good morning one and all on this wonderful day," she says as she dresses by the cast-iron wonder. "The weather feels so warm I feel like wearing summer clothes. This is the second day it feels warmer than usual. I can't figure out why it is spring in January."

Indeed, temperatures on January 11, 1888, reach above freezing, a welcome respite from the bitter cold of the new year.

Helen ambles toward the table in the kitchen. Seeing her mom, Miriam Harding, busily making breakfast and her older brother, Dennis, seventeen, and Dad, Douglas Harding, seated at the breakfast table engrossed in deep conversation, she asks, "What is this serious talk about?"

Dennis and Doug, back inside from doing chores, look up from their intense conversation just as Helen approaches. Miriam brings sausage and piping hot pancakes to the table. There is nothing better than syrup from Canada to top off the pancakes, a family favorite that brings smiles to everyone's faces.

Leaning back in his chair, Doug brushes his hair with a backward motion and locks his fingers behind his head. "We are planning how best to take advantage of the warm weather. It will be a good day to check the fences. I wonder what the weather will do. It does feel like spring, and that isn't normal for January. After all, we've had mostly double-digit below-zero temperatures this month, until yesterday."

Dennis comes up with a suggestion and says, "Dad, perhaps the weather station in Helena knows what kind of weather we can expect. They get an update from Fort Assiniboine every nine hours regarding what is happening up north. Why don't you ride Molly to Helena and pay a visit to your friend, Everett, at the telegraph office? The four and one-half mile trip will be a nice change of scenery for you." Looking at his sister, Dennis winks and adds, "Maybe his son, Tom, will be helping his dad today."

Helen glares at him and tries to hide her smile.

Miriam sets down the sausage and pancakes on the table and invites everyone to give thanks and fill their plates. Chattering about possible outdoor tasks puts the Harding family in a spirited mood. Eating together encourages conversation that sparks ideas and solutions – along with a good measure of teasing. Their words of appreciation to the cook are sincere, and everyone is fortified for the rest of the morning.

But Doug's forehead furrows as he peers out the window. He wonders how long the above-zero temperatures will last. Fort Assiniboine, located in the north-central part of Montana Territory, has a weather station inside the long brick building where telegrams about the weather are received and sent to other weather stations, including Helena. Everett G. Hobbs, Doug's friend, keeps track of the weather in Helena.

"I think I will ride to town this afternoon to catch the latest weather report," Doug says. "Dennis, you and I can check the fences this morning and then you can finish with any repairs while I'm gone. I'll be back to help finish what is left of doing chores. I'd like to know if bad weather is moving in. Miriam, you can be thinking about any staples needed for the kitchen. Helen, do you have some messages for me to deliver to anyone in town?" Doug asks with a raised eyebrow and a trace of a smile. Helen blushes.

The morning fencing project goes well. After a quick noon meal, Doug saddles up and makes the half-hour trip to Helena. Time passes quickly as Doug reminisces about life on the ranch. It's been eleven years since he and Miriam bought land and moved to Montana to build a ranch. Dennis was only six and Helen was three; how time passes.

The investment in the ranch has turned out to be a good financial decision although the family had to give up a life surrounded by people. The hardest part for Miriam is the isolation; ranches are so spread out. The closest neighbor is several miles away. The social opportunities are too infrequent for the entire family. Schooling for the children in this area doesn't exist unless someone is hired to live on the ranch to teach them. Montana Territory has not yet established an educational system in 1888. For many, attending school means paying private teachers. Some more populous communities have organized schools.

The daily routine for Helen's family revolves around farm-oriented activities. Healthy cattle are eager for their morning and evening feedings. In addition to feeding the cattle, the men check the pens for any cattle having health issues. Those that wander off by themselves, seemingly uninterested in eating, are roped and led to a nursery. An open structure with a roof provides shelter, and the animals can be more easily observed and given special attention.

These days, ranchers in Montana are forced to make adjustments to their cattle industry. The recent open-range laws of October 1886 required ranchers to put up fences to keep cattle on their property. This is a huge change. Previously, a rancher could depend on warm winds on the leeward side of the Rocky Mountains to melt the snow on the sloping plain so cattle can forage freely. Now, with no more free-range grazing, ranchers need to have hay and feed on hand.

Another change is switching from the Texas Longhorn to a hardier animal. The Hereford breed, imported from England, better fits the Montana weather. Doug knows that cattle, no matter the breed, are unlike other animals when it comes to surviving winter. The buffalo swings his massive head to clear away the snow for some blades of grass. The horse paws at the snow to find grass beneath his feet. Sheep eat snow if the water stream is covered with ice. Turkeys find a tree in which to roost rather than be buried in a drift of snow. Even chickens peck and gulp snow for life-sustaining water. But not the cow. Snow can be up to a cow's ears, and it will die of thirst.

Arriving at Helena, Doug finds the livery stable on Front Street for his horse, Molly – a place for animals to rest, drink water, and eat while their owners do business in town. Doug strolls to Main Street, where the telegraph office/weather station is located, to visit with Everett. Everett is by himself today and has a break before recording his next observation. He's happy to visit with Doug for a bit, but Doug learns little about the weather.

The incoming message from Fort Assiniboine about atmospheric conditions is unclear and difficult to understand. The report of pleasant weather preceding a drop in temperature might be useful information. But there is also something in the message about crackling static and flashes of electricity, and that wasn't making sense to anyone. They visit a bit more but Doug is eager to return to the ranch. Stopping at the General Mercantile, he buys a treat for the family. He arrives home in time to help finish with the cattle feeding. The family is pleasantly surprised with the brown paper package tied up with a string on the kitchen table – it's a taffy treat.

At bedtime, the thermometer registers a balmy 33 degrees. By the morning of January 12, it has dropped to 8 below zero. At 3 p.m., it is 18 below zero; at 10 p.m., it is 25 below. Doug recalls his visit with Everett. The report from Fort Assiniboine said there was a drop in temperature, but a 58-degree drop in twenty-four hours at the Harding Ranch seems extreme. "Why wasn't the cold wave flag flying in Helena?" he wonders. "The flag serves as a warning to prepare for cold weather. Why didn't Everett seem alarmed by any deviation from the normal observation? Did more information come in after he left?"

A cold wave warning indicates that the temperature will fall below 45 degrees and that an abnormal fall of 15 degrees or more will occur in twenty-four hours. Issuing a cold wave warning requires special procedures. Newspapers and the Associated Press wire service will receive an extra telegram when a cold wave warning is issued.

When the warning arrives, volunteers hoist and display the six-by-eight-foot white rectangular sheet with a two-foot black square in the middle. The flag flies until the volunteers are instructed by the officer in charge to take it down. Often, by the time code is transmitted and received and the message goes into effect, it is too late to help the general public.

An Arctic chill is no stranger to Montana folks; they take the winter blasts of cold, snow, and wind in stride. Surrounding states and territories look to Helena as an important indicator for their weather and prepare, at least mentally, for what might be heading their way.

As the south winds propel the warm moist air from the Gulf that Thursday morning, snowflakes, huge and billowy, come down in unending, unfurling folds from the clouds. By noon, the wind shifts suddenly to the north, increasing the gale mightily.

"From the appearance of a horizontal snowstorm and a roar that sounds like an approaching train, I'd say we have a 50-mile-an-hour wind," Doug tells Dennis. Their thoughts quickly turn to the livestock.

Despite the harsh weather conditions, Doug and Dennis bundle up and head outdoors to check on the cattle. Even with the strongest horses, Florey and Dolly, the swirling snow and forming drifts become a challenge. Checking the perimeter of the cattle pens, the men soon notice that cattle have broken through a fence. They determine that the herd is drifting with the wind. The evidence is the trampled cattle found where the fence gave way. The barbed wire barrier could not contain the frightened herd. Thoroughly chilled and wet, the men follow the fence-line home. There's little they can do in the blinding blizzard.

As afternoon and evening temperatures continue to drop, the cold, icy wind increases in speed. By evening, it storms from the northwest, plastering the ten inches of snow into drifts and against windows. Again, Dennis and Doug sit at the kitchen table to plan for the following day when, hopefully, the wind will subside. Tomorrow, they will ride to the fence-line where the cattle broke through, and then continue to look for live animals. They will be hungry and thirsty.

The following day, Friday, January 13, the wind has died. But even though the sun is out, the temperature is still extremely cold at 30 below zero. After a hearty breakfast of oatmeal with dried fruit, and a packed lunch of sausage and bread in a knapsack, the two are off. Helen is not content to stay indoors and convinces her mom that she needs to get the wagon that is on sled-like runners in the barn filled with hay to take to the surviving cattle.

Helen remembers that when cattle get out, their best workhorses, Florey and Dolly, pull the wagon of hay to where strays are. Her dad or Dennis pitch a hay trail for the cattle to follow back home. "That will work in this case, too," she tells her mom confidently. "We'll also need pickaxes, since we'll have to cut through the ice in the streams to provide water for the animals."

Dennis and Doug head southeast, the direction of yesterday's wind. As they near a ravine, they see dozens of frozen carcasses. The two men grimly survey the scene. Some cattle are frozen in an upright position. Others have stumbled, never to get up again. Sheets of ice cover their eyelids – they could not see where they were going. As the cattle drifted with the wind, the warm air from the melting snow collected around their nostrils, providing a limited source of water. But weary, blinded, and lacking nourishment, they fell victim to the storm. All are facing away from the wind. It's hard to tell how many cattle have perished, but the herd has been seriously diminished.

Dennis and Doug hope to find some surviving stray cattle in a wide swath of the area. They hope the Castle Mountains offered protection to the cattle. One can only hope. And this gives Doug an idea.

"Let's go home, take feed to the railroad terminal at Helena, rent an empty car, and fill it with hay. We'll ask the station agent if we can park the filled car on a rail siding normally used to park extra railcars."

With a plan – and a wagon already filled with hay Helen had loaded – the two men take the wagon to the Helena railroad station. The station agent agrees to rent a railcar to fill with feed, and one is reserved for the Hardings' hay. It's hard work to load the wagon with hay at home and travel the four-and-a-half miles to pitch the hay into the railcar. But they think it's worth it. Over the next few days, they take many loads of hay to Helena for potential distribution to cattle.

Ranchers in the area are notified they are welcome to take some hay if their cattle need fodder. They are also told that if cattle from the Harding Ranch appear, they should take hay from the railcar to feed them. Settlement for services will be made in spring. As expected, some very hungry and thirsty cattle are found, having traveled southeast with the wind. Many cattle are saved.

Helen had envisioned a great "save" by pitching forage to the cattle to lure them back as they follow the trail of fresh hay home. Instead, the Hardings adapt that plan and use the hay-wagon on sled-like runners to fill an empty railroad car with feed for stray livestock. The problem of getting hay to the cattle is solved.

After the cattle regain their strength, they are coaxed back home by hay pitched periodically in the snow to encourage movement back toward the ranch. The cattle follow the hay trail home, just as Helen envisioned.

❅ ❅ ❅

The memory of the January 12, 1888 blizzard endures for the community of Birney, Montana. Dessie Burnsider, a teacher in 1919, had been warned by the Birney school district patrons that if it began to snow hard to immediately dismiss school and send the pupils home.

She was told that during the memorable January 1888 blizzard, the students and teacher remained trapped at the school two nights and a day. It took that long for parents to rescue those inside the school-house.

❅　❅　❅

RECIPE
NO-BAKE HAYSTACK COOKIES
Yields 2½ dozen

UTENSILS
Bowl, medium size
Spoon to mix
Pan, medium size
Cookie sheet

INGREDIENTS
Oats (quick) 3 cups
Peanut butter 1/4 cup chunky
Butter 1/2 cup
Milk 1/2 cup
Cocoa powder 1/4 cup
Sugar 1 cup

METHOD
Mix oats thoroughly with chunky peanut butter.
Set aside.
Stir together butter, milk, cocoa, and sugar in a medium pan over
    low heat.
Whisk gently while bringing mixture to a boil.
Boil 5 minutes.
Add oats and peanut butter mixture.
Mix.
Shape teaspoon-size spoonful of mixture into a firm ball.
Place haystack cookies on a cookie sheet.
Cool haystack cookies in an icebox (refrigerator) for 30 minutes to
    set.

Mark

My name is Mark.
In this year of eighteen eighty-eight
I will be twenty-three.
This past year I filed a homestead claim
and Mae and I were married.
Today is Thursday, the twelfth of January.
It's butchering day at my bride's
home of origin. Work begins
before dawn. Large snowflakes fall.
Cleaning and scraping done,
we move inside for trimming,
chunking, and grinding.
Now at eight a.m., the sky darkens.
Temperature drops and wind picks up.
Icy particles pulverize
and cling to windows.
Family is safe inside.
We render lard, eat bismarcks, talk, and laugh.
By evening, twenty-four inches of snow accumulates.

CHAPTER FOUR

Mark from Bismarck

Located in Dakota Territory
of the United States of America

January 12, 1888
High: 2 F. (-18 C.)
Low: -25 F. (-31 C.)
Wind: NW

In 1886, Mark Manning celebrated his long-awaited twenty-first birthday. Now he had the blessing of his family to head for the world west of Bluffton, Ohio. For the past three years, "Go west, young man, go west" had been a constant drumbeat in his mind. All his thoughts centered around this momentous time of life; he would head for Bismarck in Dakota Territory. Even though his siblings – Gerhard, eighteen; Naomi, sixteen; and Frank, thirteen – would be sad to see him leave, the timing for this adventure couldn't be better.

There were three reasons his parents, George and Ruth Manning, were comfortable with Mark's plan to leave Ohio. First: In 1863, Dakota Territory had made free land available for homesteaders age twenty-one or older, so this was an opportunity. Second: The Northern Pacific Railway reached Bismarck in 1873, so the family could stay connected. Third: Sitting Bull, the great Sioux chief, had surrendered to United States troops in 1881, so the safety of their son was less of a worry for them.

In 1862, Abraham Lincoln signed the Homestead Act into law to attract settlers to the western frontier. Stipulations for obtaining free land required the individual to be at least twenty-one years of age, pay an $18 filing fee, and live on the 160 acres for five years with evidence of improvement.

"Free land, what an opportunity!" thought Mark. If land was unavailable, he'd move to Plan B. He would scout for deserted farms – surely some pioneer would have left Bismarck for opportunities even further west. If the owner had vacated, or not met the homestead requirements, there would be a deserted claim. It surely wouldn't hurt to look.

But the more he thought about it, the more Mark was unsure if the time was right to decide on a location for a homestead. Perhaps his Plan C would be the best choice for now – itinerating as a school teacher. He would have more time to find a location that would be homestead-worthy.

He had graduated from high school and attended college for one year. His parents, both teachers, often talked about their teaching experiences during meals and in the evening. He had learned something of their work. It was their life – they loved it and it appealed to him as well.

He would find a home in which to live in exchange for educating a child. He would educate a second child for free in exchange for a room to use as a classroom. He could then go door to door and gather neighborhood children and teach them for a few months. Then he would go to another part of the city and repeat the experience. He would begin at the far end of Bismarck and create employment for himself as a teacher along the railroad tracks that snaked through this growing city along the Missouri River.

And that is how Mark spent his first year away from home, as an itinerant teacher in different regions of his chosen city that he came to love. By the spring of 1887, he was at his third home, living with Edna and Daniel Unruh and their three children, Mae, eighteen; Henry, fifteen; and Evelyn, thirteen. Mark missed his family back in Ohio and his siblings were about the same ages as the Unruh children, so he enjoyed living with the family. He pitched in and helped with meal preparation and clean-up. He especially enjoyed visiting with Mae and learning all about her hopes and dreams.

Daniel works for the railroad. Edna has stayed busy at home caring for the family. They have lived in Bismarck since the year the railroad came to town in 1873, moving from New York when Mae was three. Henry and Evelyn were born in Bismarck. The Unruh family has come to know the town and its history well. Getting to know people in the greater Bismarck community has connected Mark to many people with a wide range of perspectives.

As he spent time as a teacher-in-residence with these families, Mark learned about the status of Dakota Territory. He was informed that in the 1870s, Congress had been asked to divide the territory. Urban population centers have formed in the corners of the large area, making it difficult to do business throughout the territory. Traveling north and south isn't as convenient as going east and west. In addition, the groups from the north and the south have little in common. The northern part of the territory has largely been settled by those coming from eastern and southern states, while the southern part has seen an influx of German immigrants from Russia. The people with whom Mark visited were confident that by 1889 there would be statehood for both northern and southern Dakota Territory.

He also learned that "Dakota" was the name of a tribe of Sioux Indians who had once roamed the territory. "Sioux" means "ally" or "friend." It is a fitting name, for Mark had truly found many friends in this new community.

While living with the Unruh family, Mark was increasingly attracted to their oldest daughter, Mae, with whom, he discovered, he shared many dreams. He continued his itinerant teaching, living with other families, but frequently found his way back to Mae's family for visits on weekends. As Mark and Mae spent more time together, they discussed their hopes for their future, which included homesteading together. They checked out available land for homesteading and found a location not too far from the rest of the Unruhs. Mark, in the traditional manner, asked Mae's parents for permission to marry their daughter. Unrolling a map, he added, "We'd like to homestead nearby and here is where we'd live." Of course, Mark and Mae anticipated a "yes" as Daniel and Edna seemed to really like having Mark around.

With the blessing from Mae's parents, the next item of business – that same day – was to file for a homestead. Mark's last day with his students was the last school day of September. From then on, he and Mae spent time and energy planning and building their starter home. But setting a wedding date proved to be a problem. Making improvements on the land and building a home takes time. While most weddings take place in summer or fall, it would be December before their home and yard would be ready. Not wanting to wait until next summer to get married, Mark and Mae made plans for a December wedding.

Their church didn't have space for a fellowship meal, and it would be too cold to set up tables outside as was the custom for summer and fall weddings. But Mae's parents shared an idea that might work, which the excited couple endorsed. A wedding was set for Sunday, December 11, 1887, following the church service. The family announced that the congregation would be invited to stay for the wedding service, followed by a potluck of bread, cheese and meat sandwiches. Mark's family would bring sweet cakes from Ohio.

This was a tradition going back to the Old Country. Their families had emigrated from the Netherlands to the Vistula and Elbe River area in Prussia between Germany and Poland before coming to New York. Their job had been to drain the swampy land and make it tillable, much like they had done in the Netherlands. Restrictions were placed on those working for the nobles, including limited time off for worship. With those restrictions, marriages took place following the worship service rather than on a weekday. Church families brought bread and cheese or meat to share at a noon potluck. Folks often socialized into the afternoon whether there was a wedding or not. This concept would surely work in Bismarck, they thought, and it did.

It's now January 11, a month after their wedding, and the newlyweds make a trip to Bismarck to visit Mae's parents and get supplies for the next few weeks. Her parents talk them into staying a few more days to help with the family butchering.

The Unruh family is giddy with the excitement of having everyone home. Mae's siblings, Henry and Evelyn, stay home from school for butchering day, a big, special family event.

The next morning, January 12, Edna, the keeper of tradition, is up before dawn, stirring up a batch of bismarcks for the mid-morning coffee. The recipe for jelly-filled doughnuts had been brought from the Old Country, and renamed after Chancellor Otto von Bismarck, prime minister of Prussia. In 1873, after one year of existence as Edwinton, the young Dakota Territory city had also been renamed Bismarck in hopes of attracting German investors in the railway industry.

The round jelly- or custard-filled doughnut pillows are a traditional, much-loved treat. The dough pillows are dropped into hot fat, tested for the right temperature when a half-inch square of cubed bread browns to a golden color in a minute. Brown paper wrapping, saved from a purchase at the general store, is spread out to absorb fat from the fried gems. The doughnuts are cooled for a few minutes before being jabbed in the side with a sharp knife to make an opening for filling. Once the jelly or custard is inserted, the doughnuts are elevated to the title bismarcks. The cook puts the bismarcks into a small paper bag with some sugar and shakes it ever so gently to cover evenly. Butchering day is a special occasion calling for a special treat.

January 12 starts as a good day for butchering. Activities begin before dawn. The month has been very cold up to now, and this lovely warm morning is a welcome reprieve. Anything above zero in winter is considered warm. However, as the morning progresses the weather begins to change. Dark clouds loom on the horizon.

The Unruh family is attuned to watching the weather. Daniel sometimes helps the railroad agent with telegraph logistics and transcribes Morse code for messages. He is especially interested in what he learns about the weather in Helena, Montana.

"You can almost depend on the weather in Helena arriving in Bismarck eight hours later," Daniel says.

The mess of skinning and scraping is finished by the time the temperature drops. Soon after 8 a.m., the family moves the remaining work indoors – trimming, chunking, and grinding.

Meanwhile, that sooty-looking cloud bank along the horizon creeps toward them. There is a dramatic change in temperature as it rapidly gets colder. The wind suddenly picks up, howling at an eerie pitch. Icy particles are pulverized into a fine texture and cling to the windows. It is impossible to see anything outdoors.

But indoors, butchering continues. A generous supply of wood to heat the rendering kettle has been stacked in the house in anticipation of butchering day. Chunks of lard and trimmings are put into the rendering kettle. Ribs and meaty bones are added to the mix. Family members take turns stirring the lard and fueling the fire under the oversized pot. The cooked bits of meat and browned fat are separated with a large sieve from the bubbling lard. These bits and pieces, called cracklings, are a favorite winter "stick-to-the-ribs" breakfast.

Mark has, on occasion, watched his mother-in-law prepare cracklings by warming them in her cast-iron skillet. After the morsels are heated and lard becomes liquid, the cracklings have the fat squeezed out by using a spoon to press the cracklings to the side of a bowl and drain the lard. The drained brown lard will be used on another day to bake cookies or as a spread on bread. The squeezed cracklings are returned to the iron skillet, and milk, salt, and pepper added. This mixture is cooked until the milk is absorbed. There is nothing quite like a breakfast of cracklings with rye bread and dark syrup.

Outside the Unruh home, the wind continues to howl, as twenty-four inches of snow accumulate. However, the family is together and safe, and there is plenty of food, activity, conversation, and laughter to keep them energized.

On January 12, 1888, at 8 a.m., a telegram goes from the Bismarck railway station to points beyond, describing Bismarck weather as "plummeting temperatures with increasingly violent winds." Mr. Brown, a station agent in Codington County, eastern Dakota Territory, receives the weather report, and loses no time in warning children on their way to the schoolhouse near the station that a change in weather is coming. Waving his hands wildly, he stands in the middle of the crossing and shouts, "A terrible blizzard will be here in two hours. It's the worst one of the season. Go home!" Mr. Brown repeats his message of impending doom until the children scatter. Most of them go home but, regrettably, not everyone chooses to heed the warning.

* * *

RECIPE

BISMARCKS

(Filled Doughnuts)
Deep fat fryer at 375°
Yields 2 dozen

UTENSILS
  Bowl, small size, for warm water and yeast (later add eggs)
  Bowl, medium size, for mixing
  Pans (greased) for circles of dough to rise
  Cutter, tin can, or drinking glass for cutting dough circles

INGREDIENTS
Yeast, active dry, 2 packages (about 3 t.)
Water 1/2 cup warm
Milk 1/2 cup warm
Shortening 1/3 cup
Sugar 1/3 cup
Salt 1 t.
Eggs 2
Flour 3½-4 cups
Cooking oil, additional for deep-fat frying
Jelly or custard pudding for filling

METHOD
Dissolve yeast in warm water and set aside.
Combine milk, shortening, sugar, and salt.
Add 1 cup of the flour; beat well.
Beat in softened yeast and eggs.
Add enough of remaining flour to make a moderately soft dough.
Knead 6-8 minutes until smooth.
Place in greased bowl; turn to grease surface; cover; let rise until
    double (about an hour).
Roll out on a floured surface; let it rest for ten minutes.
Roll the dough to one-third inch thick.
Dip circle cutter in flour, then press into dough.
Place dough circles on greased baking sheets.
Cover the circles of dough and let them rise until they are very
    light, 30-40 minutes.
Heat fat until a ½ inch cube of bread browns in 1 minute (375°).
Fry a few circles of dough for 1 minute on each side or until
    golden brown.
Drain on paper.
Cool for 2-3 minutes.
Cut a small slit with a sharp knife in one side of each doughnut.
Fill with about 1 t. jelly/filling.
Put some sugar and a bismarck in a paper bag; shake gently.

Paul

My name is Paul
and I was born in Cincinnati.
It's colder in Saint Paul where we now live.
Today is January twelve, eighteen eighty-eight.
I'm fourteen years old and an only child.
Before school I distribute the daily morning newspaper,
Saint Paul Globe,
to office workers at the six-story
Chamber of Commerce Building.
I learn much from my friend, Mr. Woodruff,
a weatherman in the building.
Two years ago, Father was transferred to Saint Paul
to work as a railroad traffic supervisor.
Mother makes hats when her fingers don't hurt.
Aching hands are her barometer
and tell her when a storm is coming.
It will storm says Mr. Woodruff.
It will storm says my mother.
She too is a weather forecaster.

CHAPTER FIVE

Paul from Saint Paul

Located in the State of Minnesota
of the United States of America

January 12, 1888
High: 15 F. (-9 C.)
Low: -28 F. (-32 C.)
Wind: NW

Before school on the morning of January 12, 1888, Paul, who is fourteen, walks briskly toward the southwest corner of Sixth and Robert Street. He heads toward the Chamber of Commerce Building in Saint Paul, Minnesota, where he enjoys delivering the *Saint Paul Globe* morning paper to the office workers. This newspaper has been in circulation for four years and is popular. From a distance, he sees movement on top of the Chamber Building as the anemometer, with its four little cups, catches the wind to measure the wind speed. The rain gauge and weather vane are other rooftop instruments, read at 6 a.m., 2 p.m., and 9 p.m., by Sergeant Patrick Lyons. He has collected such data for almost twenty years. Regardless of the weather, city folks can set their clocks by the regularity of Sergeant Lyons' visits.

Arriving at the front door of the Chamber of Commerce Building, Paul gazes upward at the six-story edifice, noting the fancy turret and ornate arch. It takes his breath away every time he comes to deliver the newspapers. He hurries to make his deliveries to the various offices. Something feels different today. His friend, Thomas Mayhew Woodruff, a weatherman with the United States Army, is usually waiting for weather reports to come in at this time of day, and takes time to visit with Paul. But today, Woodruff seems tense and worried as he paces back and forth in his office.

"What's going on today, Mr. Woodruff?"

"Hi, Paul. The weather today is 'a departure from normal,' as we call it. The barometer is dropping and there will be a change in weather. By the time I get the readings from other weather stations, I hardly have time to record, interpret the numbers, and prepare a map of the readings before the weather drastically changes. It is hard to know how fast this system will travel. You better hurry home and think twice about going to school – a big storm is headed this way."

Even though it seems pleasant enough, it begins to snow and Paul picks up his pace as he hurries to finish his deliveries. Back home, his mom, Deloris Petersen, arranges her work station in a spare room where she makes hats. She has a good reputation for designing and making custom hats for the millinery shop a few blocks from home. Since Paul doesn't have siblings, she uses the extra room as her workshop. While waiting for his dad, Otis Petersen, to come home from his shift at the railroad station, Paul and Deloris discuss plans for the day given Mr. Woodruff's concerns about the weather.

"It looks like staying home from school today would be the sensible thing to do as it is already snowing," agrees Deloris. "Since you won't be hurrying to school, let's make breakfast a special time."

Paul's job is setting the table, and with the decision to stay home, their schedule is more relaxed.

"Mom, did you know Mr. Woodruff has a daughter, Elizabeth, who is almost five years old? His wife, Annie, is back in Washington, D.C., waiting for Mr. Woodruff to send for her and Elizabeth. He showed me a picture of his family last week, and he really misses them. I'm glad we could move from Cincinnati to Saint Paul as a family and not have to wait for Dad to get settled in his new job as a railroad traffic supervisor. I don't see how he manages all the freight trains on the eighteen lines that go in and out of the depot each day. No wonder he is tired after his shift."

Otis arrives shortly after, and soon it is time to enjoy breakfast together. After giving thanks, he is full of questions regarding what is happening with the weather, because some of the trains haven't been arriving on time.

"Paul, what does your friend Mr. Woodruff have to say about the weather?"

"He used an official-sounding description for today," Paul says. "He called it 'a departure from normal.' Mr. Woodruff didn't seem like himself today and looked tense and worried. He told me to hurry home because a big storm is coming. He was definitely preoccupied. He paced the floor and scratched his head a lot."

Deloris, while passing the biscuits and gravy, asks Paul about Mr. Woodruff's work. "Now what is it exactly that he does?"

"He receives telegrams three times a day with temperature, barometric pressure, and wind speed and direction from forty-six stations, plus a few others, to get a more complete picture of the weather. He and his assistant, Mr. McAdie, begin at 9 a.m., to record information that arrives at his office on blank maps of the United States. The map's red lines connect stations reporting the same air pressure. It is fascinating to see the contour lines he calls isobars. Those are Greek words put together. *Iso* means equal and *baros* means weight. He showed me on the map how to recognize the high and low pressure and to find the center to anticipate the wind direction and speed. The men really concentrate since they have only one-and-a-half hours to get the information to Western Union on Fourth Street. There, the forecast is translated into Morse code and sent by wire to weather stations he calls Signal Corps offices."

"So, you learned about a barometer that measures air pressure," sighs Deloris rubbing her hands and fingers. "I too can tell if a storm is coming by my achy fingers. My doctor tells me it comes when decreased pressure of air in body cells push outward against sensitive skin."

Paul adds more, eager to share what he has learned from Mr. Woodruff. "When mercury in a barometer falls rapidly a storm usually follows, and when mercury rises in a barometer, better weather is in the forecast."

Otis seems more interested in the pressure under which Mr. Woodruff does his job than the pressure in the air or under the skin. He is curious about how Mr. Woodruff handles this line of work.

"Son, it sounds like Mr. Woodruff is under a lot of pressure to get the weather forecast right and on time. You seem to enjoy stopping by his office to visit. What have you learned about him? How did he get to be a weatherman?

"Dad, you should see the pictures in his office. There is a picture of him when he graduated from West Point – he was fifteenth in a class of forty. Then there is a picture of him as an officer in the Army. He's a first lieutenant in the Fifth Infantry. And there is another picture of his graduation from the training course in signaling, electricity, telegraphy, and the basics of physics, math, and meteorology. He knows the Morse code, and he said he'd teach me the code. He even had to take apart a telegraph transmitter to see what makes the clicking sound and put it back together again. It was perfected forty-four years ago by Mr. Morse. Isn't that something?

"You asked how he got into this line of work. He has training in following orders, he has a good education and is even a famous author. He wrote a pamphlet, *Cold Waves and their Progress*. It seems to me he gets along well with people. He often takes time to visit with me; I think it's because he misses his family. Since he was doing a good job in Washington, D.C., the government officers asked him to start a branch in Saint Paul so that people would get the weather forecast two to five hours earlier."

"Paul, I don't remember hearing you talk about your friend at the Chamber building until recently. Has he been in our city long?" Deloris asks.

"He told me this branch office opened October 20 of last year, with the first forecast issued eight days later. First of all, though, they had to create Mr. Woodruff's job. I found out five businessmen from the Meteorological Committee of Saint Paul Chamber of Commerce went to Washington, D.C. These men all have offices in the building where I deliver newspapers. They convinced people in Washington to set up a weather forecasting station in Saint Paul. They told the officials it would be good for business to warn people ahead of time if bad weather was coming their way."

The Petersen family enjoys their meal and catching up with each other's activities. They take their dishes to the kitchen, and thank the cook. Deloris reminds Otis that Paul will be around today. Otis says he will likely go back to his office at the railroad after a few hours of rest.

"Paul," says Deloris, "let's make a snack today – GORP, the Good Old Raisins and Peanuts recipe, and we can add whatever we like.

"That sounds great," Paul responds. "Let's make it a fun day of games, writing, drawing, and snacking – sort of like the Christmas break."

Meanwhile, back at the Chamber of Commerce Building, Woodruff is observing the weather maps, noting that warmer temperatures have occurred before a rapid drop in temperatures at both Fort Assiniboine and Helena. This gives him pause. He has never seen this before. The January 12 report from Helena shows the mercury reached 40.5 degrees above zero at midnight and then plummeted 66.5 degrees, to 26 below zero. This is unprecedented for a twenty-four-hour period. Everett G. Hobbs reports from Helena, and he is quite reliable. There must be an explanation for this out of the ordinary drop in temperature from Helena. Perhaps the reporting from Fort Assiniboine is an error showing a drop of 24 degrees overnight when in reality it was more. Maybe a lazy observer, who for convenience sake, fabricated the report. He has witnessed firsthand the occasional non-professional approach to reporting at some of the outposts.

Having issued weather reports for only a short time in Saint Paul, Woodruff reminds himself that he has posted more cold wave warnings during the past ten weeks than Washington, D.C., issued the entire past year. Eyebrows have been raised at his frequent calls for a "cold wave."

As the author of the pamphlet *Cold Waves and their Progress*, which he wrote in 1885, Woodruff is considered an expert. In Washington, Acting Chief Signal Officer Brigadier General Adolphus W. Greely relies on information from Woodruff's pamphlet. A cold wave means the temperature will fall below 45 degrees, and an abnormal fall of at least 15 degrees will occur in twenty-four hours. Greely is an uncompromising, tough commander who governs by rigid enforcement of rules and orders. Woodruff, trained in military protocol, does not want to aggravate Greely, and he wants to be sure of his predictions.

It's been twenty-four hours since the storm hit Helena, preceded by warm weather and followed by large snowflakes. The plummeting temperature and sudden winds made visibility impossible. The high for Helena on January 11 had been 38.5 at 10 p.m., before it dropped to 26 below zero the next day. But not wanting to cry "wolf" when there may not be danger of a cold spell, Woodruff decides to be cautious. It doesn't help that information arrives at the Saint Paul office only every eight hours. He fears retribution from Washington and decides to not issue a cold wave warning.

Many scenarios flit through Woodruff's mind as he begins to second-guess his decision. There is the uncertainty of statistical information not being 100 percent correct. Then there is the possibility of false reporting from the outposts. How can predictions be certain with this unusual weather? Thinking about his decision is exhausting and renders Woodruff frozen with inaction regarding the impending threatening weather. But it takes only a moment to rouse himself out of complacency and back to his usual self. He will issue a cold wave warning, even if it is late. If his supervisor thinks this warning is unnecessary, so be it.

But Woodruff's cold wave warning for Saint Paul on January 12 comes too late for many. The high is 15 degrees at midnight. By nightfall, the barometer falls to 29.48 and the temperature quickly plummets to 28 below zero. Deloris' fingers and hands ache as air pressure pushes the cells outward, causing pain to sensitive tissues. Otis is beside himself, with trains running from one to fifteen hours behind schedule.

To be sure, this is no baby blizzard that rolls out of the cradle on the leeward side of the Rockies. The immense irregular wall of the Rocky Mountains squeezes and deflects the air currents, altering temperatures and air pressure. Consistently, warmer temperatures precede snowfall in Edmonton, Saskatoon, Helena, Bismarck, and Saint Paul prior to the arrival of sudden Arctic hurricane-like winds. This storm is a full-grown monster.

Paul remains at home the rest of Thursday and again on Friday, January 13. His active imagination finds an outlet through pen and paper. He writes, "The winds blow with force through cave-like nostrils of a mighty mythic being in convulsions – churning, grinding, and swirling the snow into a gritty, icy, flour-like texture." He can hardly wait to begin drawing this figment of his imagination.

It is Saturday before Paul attempts going to the Chamber of Commerce Building. After several days at home, he is ready to get out and distribute his papers. Paul reads with interest the front page of the morning edition of the *Saint Paul Globe*. The paper includes a number of stories about the major winter storm that has moved across the northern plains of the United States. There is an article about "Casualties Reported in Dakota, Nebraska, Iowa, and Minnesota," but the bold headline "STUNG TO DEATH: Several Persons Put to Sleep Forever by the Blizzard's Viper Tongue" inspires him to play with creating yet another one-of-a-kind drawing.

❊ ❊ ❊

Woodruff's message arrives late in some places on January 12, 1888. Perhaps there is a backup at the local Western Union office. Perhaps the cold wave flag didn't fly; maybe there is no volunteer available to raise it. Some may not know the meaning of that flag. Only those who are nearby will see the white cloth with a black square in the middle and, hopefully, they understand the warning that cold weather is coming. Visibility may be hampered. Some will be unable to see the white flag with the wind churning up the snow.

Some question the effectiveness of flying the cold wave flag. Settlers out in the wide-open spaces, who are acquainted with the elements, learn survival skills by preparing for and accommodating the weather conditions. They trust their instincts.

❊ ❊ ❊

See Addenda for Chapter Five: "Weather Maps"

❊ ❊ ❊

RECIPE
GORP

(Good Old Raisins and Peanuts)
MAKE TO TASTE

UTENSILS
  Medium-size bowl
  Spoon for stirring
INGREDIENTS
  Raisins
  Peanuts
  Fruit, dried
  Candy pieces
  Chocolate chips, semi-sweet
METHOD
  Mix desired portions of selected ingredients.

Maria

My name is Maria.
I married John Jac when sixteen.
Our first three babies died in the old country.
We came to America on the ship *City of Richmond*.
Three days before docking in New York City
Johann was born.
Four years later in Dakota Territory his brother,
Peter, arrived. In three years Anna came. After another three
years Jacob arrived and in two years, Julius was born.
The January twelve, eighteen eighty-eight blizzard
changed families forever.
That day Peter stayed home and Johann went to school.
Johann, at age thirteen, froze to death in the blizzard
along with four schoolmates ages seven to sixteen.
They became separated from Mr. Cotton, the teacher;
he was boarding with us.
I weep for the families of the five frozen sons,
our family included.
We are families of the prairie.
Our sons died on the Dakota Plains, in Dakota Territory.
My heart is heavy with grief.

CHAPTER SIX

Maria or Mariean from Freeman

Located in Dakota Territory of the United States of America

January 12, 1888
High: 26.8 F. (-2 C.)
Low: -14 F. (-23 C.)
Wind: NW

Maria is emphatic. "No," she tells her two oldest sons, nine-year-old Peta (Peter) and thirteen-year-old Johann (John). "You cannot go to school today and that is final!"

The calm weather of January 12, 1888, does not feel right to her. There is foreboding in the air. "And besides," she says, "there is a small sooty-looking cloud on the horizon. Whenever I have seen that kind of cloud, a bad storm is brewing!"

Maria's husband, Johann (John Jac, whose father was Jacob) Albrecht, who is more easy-going, feels he needs to guard his sons from

Maria's over-protectiveness. He counters, "I don't see anything wrong with the boys going to school if they want to, my dear Mariean. They'll be all right. They are quite grown-up, you know."

And with the boys' father swaying the decision in favor of them going to school if they want, they decide that John will go and Peter will stay home to please his mother. The family gathers around the table for breakfast. John and Peter have three younger siblings: Anna, six; Jacob, three; and Julius, one day short of being a one-year-old. Julius sits in his high chair grinning from ear to ear. He likes the attention from his older siblings.

The Albrecht family, together with many of their neighbors, came to the southeastern part of Dakota Territory from Volhynia, a province in Russia, in 1874. The Albrechts provide room and board to Mr. James P. Cotton, the schoolteacher. He has eaten breakfast and is ready to leave for school across the section to the west. The two other families living nearest the school have more children in their respective households than the Albrecht family. That is why the Albrecht family agreed to house the schoolteacher. The Albrecht family lives near the eastern edge of the same square-mile section as the schoolhouse.

Two other families reside near the Rosefield District No. 66 schoolhouse. Johann and Anna Schrag Kaufman and their seven children live one-half mile south and across the road to the west from the school. The Peter O. Graber family lives north, a stone's throw from the school. They also arrived on the Dakota plains with their seven children in 1874. But Peter's wife, Freni, died May 25, 1875, after being in America less than a year. On June 18 of the same year – twenty-four days later – Peter married Susanna Gering, also from Volhynia. The new bride gained not only a husband, but also an instant family of seven children, the youngest two years old. By 1888, seven more children had been added to the family. Their home is full and overflowing.

Mr. Cotton, the teacher at Rosefield District No. 66, is aware of the tension in the Albrecht home regarding school attendance that morning. He calls back over his shoulder to John and Peter in English, "I hope you boys will not be absent!"

The teacher speaks only English. The children's parents, Maria and John Jac, speak a Swiss-German or "Schweitzer-Deutch" dialect, as do the other families. The dialect has its roots in Switzerland, where it was influenced by Germans living nearby. Their ancestors traveled across Europe in search of religious freedom; they arrived in Russia in the 1770s.

The Volhynian families are a close-knit group, having come from several different villages in Russia where they lived near each other. Visitations were frequent there, especially in winter, with sleighs leaving paths connecting the Swiss-German communities.

John Jac Albrecht, from the village of Kotosufka in Volhynia Province of Russia, married Maria Graber from the village of Horodisch on July 9, 1866. He was nineteen and she had recently turned sixteen. After almost three years of marriage, their firstborn arrived, but lived only seven-and-a-half months. The next two siblings also had short lives. Having buried all three of their children in Volhynia, John Jac and Maria were overcome with sadness.

Adding to their sadness and worry was the 1870 edict from the czar. Their community was forewarned that new regulations would be implemented within ten years: children in school would be taught in Russian; men must serve in the military; churches and schools would be Russianized. Moving to America seemed like the best option for the Albrechts and the other community members. Scouts sent to America reported that there was land available in Dakota Territory. Preparing for a journey and a new life in Dakota Territory became all-consuming. By 1874, arrangements had been made for visas and passports, and land and belongings were sold.

The timing wasn't the best for the Albrechts – Maria was pregnant. But the hope of new life within her and the opportunity to worship freely, as was their custom, gave Maria the incentive she needed to look ahead. "New beginnings are indeed possible," she thought. Maria gave birth to Johann, (John), August 28, 1874, aboard the ship, *City of Richmond*, three days before arriving at the New York harbor. The sweet contentment of their baby was a reminder of the blessing and the fragility of life.

On the same ship were Johann and Anna Schrag Kaufman, from the villages of Horodisch and Waldheim respectively. They had buried their four-year-old son in Volhynia and were also looking for a new start in America with their two other sons. And then the unthinkable happened: their one-year-old died on the ship and was buried at sea, his body lowered into the murky waters of the Atlantic Ocean.

Anna resisted the bitterness in her heart by practicing gratitude. While she grieved the loss of her two sons, she was grateful for her three-year-old, Johann (John). She helped Maria with child care as much as possible. Caring for a baby helped soothe the ache in her heart.

Peter O. Graber was from the village of Horodisch. His two wives – Freni Gering, who died after being in America less than a year, and Susanna Gering, his second wife – had roots in the Waldheim community of the Volhynia region.

Now living in America, community life for the Albrechts and their neighbors centers around weekly gatherings at the church, where services are conducted in High German, functions are celebrated in connection with the English school, and they converse in their dialect when helping each other.

It is children from these three families – the Albrechts, Grabers, and Kaufmans – who attend Rosefield School District No. 66 on this fateful day, January 12, 1888. They include John Albrecht, thirteen (who was born on the ship); Peter, sixteen; and John Graber, fourteen (both Freni's sons); Andrew Graber, eleven (Susanna's son); and brothers John, sixteen; Henry, ten; and Elias Kaufman, seven. At school, Mr. Cotton calls the children by their English names. At home their German names are used: Johann, Peta, Andreas, Heinrich, and Aleas.

While the morning begins mild and balmy, the weather changes dramatically around 11 a.m. The sudden noise of the wind, the increasing darkness, the windows plastered with dirty snow, and the snow sifting through every crack of the uninsulated school structure is unnerving for everyone. Mr. Cotton knows that lessons are over. There is no indication of the storm letting up. Mr. Cotton asks the oldest two boys for their thoughts on whether to stay at school or brave the elements to go to the nearest home; the Grabers live within shouting distance on a calm day. The sixteen-year-old boys, Peter Graber and John Kaufman agree: "Stay at the school!"

They have heard more conversations regarding weather from their parents than Mr. Cotton will ever hear. Staying put until someone comes to look for the missing has been drilled into them. Yet Mr. Cotton questions the sustainability of keeping warm and going without food for who knows how long. Already, keeping the fire going isn't working well. Given the circumstances, the oldest two boys consent to everyone walking to the Grabers' place. After all, they live just a hop and a skip north of the school, so it won't take long to get there.

Mr. Cotton and the students leave the school and head into the storm. But they are not dressed for the bitter cold and wind. The boys had all left home that mild morning wearing only light jackets over their plaid flannel shirts and one-piece cotton long johns under their clothes. Henry and Elias are used to wearing John's hand-me-downs –

the shirts are getting a bit thin from both wear and being washed with homemade lye soap. The Kaufman boys didn't bother with mittens and caps today, leaving them even more exposed to the elements. The youngest of the group, ages ten and seven, are the most vulnerable to the sub-zero weather because of their small bodies.

John Albrecht, who is thirteen and the oldest in his family, considers himself almost as grown up as John Kaufman and Peter Graber, the sixteen-year-old fellows. He falls in line with the older group as do John Kaufman's brothers Henry, ten, and Elias, seven. "Stick together if you are in trouble!" – the indelible message from their parents keeps playing over and over in the Kaufman children's heads. However, the oldest boys confidently set the pace, with John Kaufman making sure his siblings stay together. John Albrecht, having no other family members at school that day since Peter stayed home, latches on to the oldest boys and helps with the little ones in that lineup.

The Graber siblings get separated when the drifts become too much for Andrew. He calls for Peter, his half-brother, five years older, for help. But Peter, too far ahead or because of the pelting ice and wind, can't hear and continues his pace. However, John, his other half-brother, who is three years older, and Mr. Cotton hear his plea and soon appear. Mr. Cotton calls for the other five boys to wait. There is no answer. "Perhaps they are already at your house," Mr. Cotton tells the two Graber boys. "Your brother, Peter, will know the way to his home," he adds reassuringly.

But the five boys in the lead – John Albrecht, Peter Graber, and the Kaufman brothers, Elias, Henry, and John, who set out walking directly into the wind – unknowingly change direction and travel southeast with the wind and away from the Graber home. Snow, wind, ice, and exhaustion can be disorienting. Their trek takes them farther and farther from their destination and their bodies become increasingly weary and cold. The temperature keeps dropping as the day wears on. Soon they are aware they have become separated from the others.

Meanwhile, John and Andrew Graber, led by Mr. Cotton, put their heads down and set one foot in front of the other as they walk into the northwest wind. After a time of staggering into the formidable wind, Mr. Cotton becomes unsure of where he is and comes to a halt. "Have we missed the farmhouse?" he shouts.

Squinting through his partially frozen eyelids and looking around in confusion, he tries to get his bearings. They should have been to the house by now. Just then there is a brief lull in the force of the wind.

All three see saplings sticking up from the ground, and then all know instinctively where they are. The young shelter belt saves them. They have begun drifting east of the farmstead, but now – by following the saplings – they soon reach Andrew and John's home. By this time, Andrew is no longer feeling the cold as a feeling of warmth spreads throughout his body.

They have a joyous reunion at the Graber home but quickly realize the other five children aren't there. Susanna, with both gratitude and fear clutching her heart, begins treating Andrew for frostbite. The home remedy of the day is to rub snow on the frozen extremities to bring back circulation, but going outside for snow is out of the question. So she thaws his fingers and toes first in cool and then warm water so as not to shock the body even more. Wrapping Andrew in a blanket, Susanna then prepares hot chocolate milk to warm everyone on the inside. This is a treat usually reserved for special occasions and their safe arrival in this weather certainly is special.

At the Albrecht home, the family is worried, yet also comforted that the teacher, Mr. Cotton, who boards with them, has not come home. Assuming he and the students must have stayed at the schoolhouse helps relieve their concern. They will wait until morning, when the wind dies down, to go to the schoolhouse. While their plan for the next morning eases their minds, their hearts ache for the missing ones. The family wonders: "is everyone alright?"

Maria thinks about Julius, who will have his first birthday the following day. The children will surely all want to be present. She is planning to make his birthday special for the family and has settled on making *mak kuchen* (poppyseed pie). *Mak kuchen* is a family favorite, baked much like a custard pie, but with a sweet dough rather than a pie dough. In spring, the tiny black poppy seeds brought along to Dakota Territory from Russia are sown, and then harvested in summer with some saved for seed for the following spring. Maria falls into a fitful sleep, planning for Julius' birthday and worrying about her Johann.

The Kaufman family also believes their sons have stayed at school. When nighttime comes, and there still is no sign of the three schoolboys, they are quite sure that in the morning there will be a reunion at the schoolhouse. In the meantime, the family will wait, pray, and hope the children stay together in a place of shelter as they have been told to do on many occasions.

Friday, January 13, dawns. The storm has let up enough so Mr. Cotton walks the short distance to the school, anticipating that John

Jac Albrecht and Johann Kaufman will come to the school looking for their boys, which they do. "Where are our boys?" the two fathers ask in unison, repeating the question as they look around hoping that from somewhere their sons will appear.

Mr. Cotton, with grief in his voice, says, "The boys are not here." And then the teacher relates the decision-making process and the reason for leaving the school and how they become separated. They retrace the steps to the place where Andrew called for help. The fathers look for possible evidence of where they may have walked but find nothing. Word of the missing children spreads in the community and many come to help look, but by nightfall there still is no sign of the five missing boys. On Saturday, another search takes place, repeating the efforts of the previous day – again without finding the missing ones.

Sunday comes and all three families attend Salem Church with their children except for the missing five: John Albrecht, Peter Graber, the three Kaufman boys, John, Henry, and Elias. The Salem Church is located across the section west from the Kaufman family. The Graber boys, John and Andrew, having made it through the storm, hope they won't be peppered with questions. It is hard to remember the details. What they really remember – and can still feel – are the cold, icy needles of snow penetrating their clothing and pelting their exposed and sensitive skin.

Reverend Christian Mueller and Reverend Christian Kaufman conduct the morning worship service. As the service progresses, the church door opens and a man comes in, removes his hat, and finds a place to sit in the back row. During the closing hymn, the eyes of worshipers follow this man as he makes his way to the front of the sanctuary where the aged former preacher, Johann Schrag, is standing and singing with the congregation. Reverend Schrag recognizes the man as Johann Goertz, a neighbor living a mile-and-a-half from him; they are the same age and emigrated the same year, but from different places. Mr. Goertz whispers into his neighbor's ear in High German. The former preacher motions to the current preachers to come to where the two of them are standing. Mr. Goertz repeats his message to the preachers and returns to his seat. Following the benediction, the congregation is asked to be seated for an announcement.

The worship leader from the ministerial team says, "Our neighbor, Johann Goertz, who lives three miles to the east, has come to inquire about missing children." A gasp and then a hush falls over the congregation and the minister continues. "This morning, his sons discovered five frozen bodies of children on the farm, but Mr. Goertz and his sons don't know to whom they belong."

The three fathers of the missing boys immediately go over to where Mr. Goertz is sitting and start asking questions. Mr. Goertz explains, "My sons, Peter, seventeen, and Henry, fifteen, were out choring this morning and checking the yard. They saw an arm extending upward from the snow. This caught the boys' attention. After brushing off the snow, they found five frozen bodies of children, but they didn't know who they were. The boys then came to the house to tell me and my wife about the discovery, and I went out to have a look."

The Goertz family members speak the Low German dialect in their home and High German at church. The Goertz family doesn't go to their church service regularly in winter as the building is more than five miles away, which is why the family happens to be home this Sunday morning. Since the boys attend school at District No. 15 of Marion Township they don't recognize the frozen children from church or school.

After seeing the frozen boys for himself, Mr. Goertz wonders what he should do. He doesn't recognize any of the children either. Although it's too late for the beginning of the Salem Church service three miles to the west, he dresses in his Sunday best and goes to the church anyway. Perhaps he can visit with the worshipers in attendance before they go home; maybe someone knows something about the missing children. The boys proceed to hitch up the horse and sleigh for their father.

At the church, and after visiting with Mr. Goertz following his startling report, the three fathers of the missing boys plan to determine if the frozen children in Goertz's yard are their sons. The three families live in both a state of hope that their sons have been found and denial, believing the missing boys are still alive somewhere. Johann Schrag, the former preacher, is also very much interested in what Mr. Goertz has to say as the three missing Kaufman boys are his grandsons; Anna, the boys' mother, is his daughter.

The fathers decide what will be needed to retrieve the children – if theirs – from Mr. Goertz's yard. The wives and children are taken home and the fathers take what they need and head to the Goertz farm. There they discover the frozen children are indeed their sons, their bodies encased in a frozen sculpture. In their Swiss-German dialect, the men unleash the pain in their hearts with moans and words of grief. Johann Kaufman cries out, "O God, is it my fault or yours that I find my three boys frozen here like the beasts of the field?"

The men go to work, prying the children free from the frozen snow and ice. John Kaufman, who is sixteen, has his arm around his seven-year-old brother, Elias, and they are bound together in a frozen block. Nearby is their brother, ten-year-old Henry, on his knees either praying or having become too tired to get up. The men work together to load the frozen children onto their respective sleighs.

The fathers feel the depth of each other's loss and pain as they lift each other's children onto the sleighs. Johann Kaufman and Peter O. Graber help John Jac Albrecht lovingly guide his thirteen-year-old son's frozen body onto the Albrecht sleigh. Peter O., who has not experienced the death of any of his fourteen children before this, weeps inconsolably as the other two fathers help him lift his beloved sixteen-year-old, Peter, onto his sleigh. The children are transported to their respective homes, where their bodies will be thawed for burial. Each father makes his way to his own farm, wondering how his family will cope with the reality of death.

Maria wipes her tears with a handkerchief in one hand, then places it over her mouth to muffle her cry of despair as she opens the door. John Jac Albrecht's sad eyes meet Maria's as he carries in their oldest son's body, frozen in a fetal position. They are reminded of the three lifeless children in Volhynia whom they also carried into the main room of their home to prepare them for burial. John Jac places the stiff, rock-hard body close to the stove to thaw. The four siblings stare at the corpse. Peter, nine, and Anna, six, hold hands. Jacob, three, and Julius, the newly turned one-year-old, cling to Maria.

A mile away, the Graber household solemnly makes space near the fire in their home for Peter's frozen body. Both John and Andrew have the realization of, but not the words to express, the sense of "but for the grace of God, it could be me." They numbly gaze at the thawing form by the stove. The other children quiet themselves in the background, as they are growing up in an era of "being seen and not heard."

When John Kaufman brings the frozen remains of his and Anna's three sons into the house, he does not expect what comes next. Having already released three sons to death, one in Volhynia, one on the ship, and one during the first year of living in this new world, Anna is faced with saying good-bye to three more sons. Her mind and heart cannot bear the shock of this tragedy. She bursts into unstoppable laughter. This continues, in episodes of sudden, uncontrollable, and inappropriate laughter. Amidst the peals of laughter, John feels overwhelmed; his load seems almost unbearable. He too, has now lost six sons. He needs to care for Julius, five; Jonathan, three; and Emma, one. There are plans to make for the funeral service. When and how, he wonders, will the burial take place?

Days later, the five boys, now thawed, are fitted into coffins, although with difficulty. Following the memorial service at the church, they are buried in a single grave at the cemetery near the church (which would later be known as Salem-Zion Mennonite Church).

❄   ❄   ❄

Today, a marker at the frozen boys' grave acknowledges their story.

❄   ❄   ❄

Anna Kaufman likely experienced a mild response of pseudobulbar effect displacement, a condition that affects the way the brain controls emotions. This may occur when a person cannot deal directly with a shocking situation. In the case of this tragedy, Anna's emotions overcompensated with an inappropriate response. In time, as reality set in, so did Anna's acceptance of the tragedy.

Anna's husband, John, died in 1890 at age forty-five of a broken heart. They had been married twenty-four years. Anna remarried, moved to Kansas, and started a new chapter. Her sorrows weren't over: her son Julius died in Kansas at the age of twenty, likely of a ruptured appendix. Anna died in 1930 on her eighty-first birthday.

John Jac Albrecht and Maria were married a few weeks shy of sixty-seven years. John died in 1933 at the age of eighty-six, and Maria nine months later at eighty-three.

Peter O. and Susanna Graber were married twenty-two years. Peter O. died in 1897 at sixty-seven and Susanna in 1913 at sixty-three.

❄   ❄   ❄

Funerals in 1888 were held without the service of morticians. Bodies were readied for burial at home. A wooden box was fashioned for a casket and relatives, neighbors, and friends helped dig the grave. The body was kept in the home a day and night or two before burial. Called a wake, it gave loved ones opportunity to pay their respect and comfort the family. Following the memorial service, horse-drawn buggies, wagons, or bobsleds would proceed to the cemetery for burial.

❋ ❋ ❋

RECIPE
KUCHEN
(Sweet Dough Pie)
Bake at 350° for 30 minutes, or until a knife
inserted in the middle comes out clean.

UTENSILS
Pie plate (greased)
Bowl, small size, to mix filling
Bowl, small size, for sliced fruit

INGREDIENTS
Eggs 2
Sugar 1 cup
Flour 2 T.
Salt 1/4 t.
Cream (sweet) or half cream and half milk 3/4 cup
Fruit cut-up 1¼ cups or *poppyseed roll filling

METHOD
Roll out dough VERY THIN using a small portion of a yeast
sweet dough.
Put into a greased pie plate.
Mix the ingredients and warm or partially cook (except for the
fruit which is kept at room temperature).
Arrange fruit evenly on the dough.
Pour the warm/heated filling onto the fruit in the pie plate.
Sprinkle with cinnamon or nutmeg if desired.
*For a poppyseed kuchen, use 1/3 cup of poppyseed roll filling
and mix with the ingredients instead of using the cut-up fruit.

*POPPYSEED ROLL FILLING
Mix 1½ cups poppyseed, ground, 1¼ cups sugar and 1 heaping T.
flour.
Add 1¼ cups boiling water (part cream may be used).
Boil, stirring constantly.
Cool – if it seems too thick, add a little water or cream.

Katharina

My name is Katharina and I am eleven, almost twelve years old.
It's January twelve, eighteen eighty-eight, a calm, beautiful day.
My brothers, Peter, nine, and Isaac, five, and I
beg to go by sleigh to visit John W.,
our brother, and his family.
They live east, across the field, and past the timber claim
one and one-half miles from our home,
in a sod house.
Two mules are hitched to the sleigh.
Our hired hand navigates.
Our nephew, a toddler, likes the *reescha tweeback*,
roasted double-decker buns, we bring.
Mid-afternoon a sudden change in weather occurs;
we prepare to go home.
The sleigh is piled with blankets.
It becomes dark; calm changes to storm;
swirling snow blinds man and beast.
The driver can't see; mules are given free rein.
The animals tire, stop near a haystack, and won't continue.
We find protection in the haystack.
After a while, we hear our names; it is Father calling.
We answer; Father leads the mules and us in the sleigh
along the fence-line home.
Mother has a lamp in the window.
We see, we are grateful, we embrace.
All gather around the hearth of home.

CHAPTER SEVEN

Katharina or Katharine from Henderson
AND
Lena from East of Henderson

Located in Nebraska of the United States of America

January 12, 1888
High: 31 F. (0 C.)
Low: -4 F. (-20 C.)
Wind: N

*This chapter begins and ends with stories
told by eleven-year-old girls.*

Katharina's Story

M y name is Katharina Friesen. I am eleven years old; I'll be twelve in a few weeks. My parents are Jacob and Anna Friesen. I answer to different names. When, about three years ago, my oldest brother, John W., married Katharina Dick, it got confusing with two Katharinas in the same family. So at home my name is shortened to Katharine or Tine (Teen). And now that John W. and Katharina's toddler, John A., is talking, I am *Taunta* Tine to my nephew. *Taunta* means aunt.

53

My shortened name of Katharine makes me think of stories my parents told me about Catherine the Great from Russia. She was an empress who came from Germany. Since she wanted to make the land in Russia good farmland, she chased away people they called Turks and invited my great-great-grandparents from Prussia. That land is in Europe and close to Germany. She wanted to have them become farmers in Russia. She also invited other people who spoke German. It was a good deal for them, as land in Prussia was expensive.

Catherine the Great promised free land, tax exemptions, and freedom if they would come. They could have their own churches and schools, and keep speaking German. And the men wouldn't have to fight in the Russian army. After Catherine the Great died, things began to change. In the 1870s, Czar Alexander had different ideas. He said everyone would have to start speaking in Russian everywhere – including in the churches and schools. And men would have to join the Russian army.

That was when my parents and others decided to think about moving to America. They came to Nebraska in 1874, where I was born three years later. I want to tell you about life in America, especially one day in particular.

January 12, 1888, started out as a beautiful calm day with about two feet of snow on the ground. My younger brothers, Peter, who was nine, and Isaac, who was five, and I begged Mom and Dad to let us visit our oldest brother, John W., and his family. They live across the field and past the woods – my father says it's a timber claim. They live in a sod house one and one-half miles east from our home. I wanted to play with John W. and Katharina and little John A. You probably wonder why we weren't in school.

Our father, for some reason of his own, was slow in sending his children to an English school. In earlier years, a lady named Fannie White taught English school in spring in a sod house one mile north of Henderson on Peter Wolf's land. My older brothers and sister went there only a short time, three days to be exact. They liked the German school in homes much better.

People let them have school in their homes for part of one year and then someone else lets them use their home for part of the next year. My folks said about eighteen homes in the community have been used for school at one time or another during the first thirteen years in America. The favorite three-month German school for John W., Anna, and Jacob J., my older brothers and sister, was about three miles away in a small room at Benjamin Ratzlaff's home. They really liked their teacher, Cornelius Heinrichs. He was friendly and funny. He played with the students at recess and made school fun. They said he never scolded or "used the rod" like so many teachers did when students were naughty. Mr. Heinrichs didn't agree with the "No Licking, No Learning" motto.

Some families do some homeschooling, which means reading from the German Bible, memorizing Bible verses, and beginning the Fiebel or the ABCs. My brother, John W., is teaching himself to read English, and my brother, Jacob J., is really interested in education. He's even taken some college courses. Peter went to school only a little while, but is already teaching himself to read English. And Isaac, at age five, is too young to go to school.

My mother needs me a lot around the house since my sister, Anna, who is named after Mother, is helping other families whenever there is a new baby in their home. Anna's getting married this summer. I'm so excited. I have been helping my mother with cleaning baby furniture so I wouldn't be surprised if we'd have another baby in our family soon. So far there is no schooling for me, as Mother can't get along without me.

My brother, John W., and sister, Anna, didn't go to school for a time either, because they were needed at home. They watered and cared for all the trees Dad and my brothers planted shortly after they got to America. Dad explained it was because of the Timber Culture Act of 1873. The government would give him 160 acres if he planted forty acres of trees and took care of them. The trees needed a lot of care. When the trees were planted, there was no time for schooling – only watering and hoeing.

Dad said the rules changed to only having to plant ten acres of trees. But you still had to plant at least 2,700 trees no farther apart than twelve feet. Some of the trees died and had to be replaced, but as long as at least 675 lived, it was okay. Eight years after Dad started the program, they sent two people to check to make sure we were taking good care of the trees.

The trees are in rows. And even though there can't be more than twelve feet between the rows or the trees, there's room for a horse to pull a wagon with a water barrel. That makes the watering chore much easier. It also gives us a shortcut across the section that we use whenever we visit John W. and his family. And whenever he goes to town, John W. and his neighbors also use that shortcut. It's much easier for the horses because they don't have to go over the steep incline of the railroad tracks.

John Boldt, our hired hand, hitched a team of mules to a sleigh and took us children to my brother's home. Mom sent along some *reesche tweeback*, roasted double-decked buns, to share with my brother's family. These buns are shaped with a smaller ball of dough on top of the bottom larger ball of dough, and then baked. She makes them every Saturday, and if any are still left on Monday, we separate them and toast them on a cookie sheet. Because they stay good for a long time, my parents brought this food with them when they came to America.

The day with John W. and Katharina and the baby passed quickly. Around mid-afternoon, the wind arose very suddenly, swirling snow around. It got dark and loud rumbling sounds came from somewhere. The change in weather was very scary for all of us. Mr. Boldt, the hired hand, and John W. quickly hitched up the mules and Katharina got extra blankets. She packed Peter, Isaac, and me in the sleigh and we left for home.

The snow was blinding and guiding the mules was impossible. So the hired hand gave the team free rein. He figured they would know the way home. Mules sense direction and sure enough, they headed for home. They made it through the woods and kept on going.

But the pelting ice, swirling snow, and bitter cold was frightening. My brothers and I buried ourselves deeper underneath the heavy blankets that John W. and Katharina had sent. Then all of a sudden, the mules stopped. We were by a haystack and the mules seemed to have no intention of going any farther. It was common to have hay stacked close to the edge of the field so it could be hauled in as needed.

Since we were stopped there, we made a cave in the haystack and crawled into it for protection. Even the mules stuck in their heads.

Meanwhile, my worried father went into the storm to look for us. He followed the barbed wire fence for one-half mile and kept calling for us by name. He was exhausted, but he continued walking and calling, hoping we would hear him.

We finally heard his voice, and all of us shouted, "Here we are, Daddy!"

We were so glad to see him. He put us in the sleigh and then Mr. Boldt helped lead the mules that were pulling the sleigh. One rein was fastened to Dad, who held onto the barbed wire fence, following it all the way home. He told us to watch for a light coming from our house, as Mother had placed a lamp in the window. When we finally saw it, we were so excited and we shouted, "We're home! We're home!" It felt so good to be safe at home and out of the storm.

I may not be a student in a classroom, but I am a student of experience. I will never forget this lesson of being prepared for whatever can happen. It will be with me always. I'll never leave home in a sleigh without a blanket.

✳   ✳   ✳

Katharina maintained an interest in weather all her life. With a worried demeanor, she frequently peered out of the kitchen window to watch for unusual cloud formations.

✳   ✳   ✳

According to Dulcie, the correspondent for the "Henderson Clippings" section of the *York Republican*, the temperature on Sunday, January 15, 1888, was 35 degrees below zero. Trains stopped running January 12-15, partially because of the snowstorm and partially because of a wreck west of Henderson. Trainmen were thrown to the ground, and the engineer had slight injuries. Drifts in places were ten feet high. However, where it was level, the snow was great for sleighing.

✳   ✳   ✳

Martha Friesen, writer of "Centennial Clippings" in the *Henderson News* for December 31, 1987, quotes T.J. Fiegenbaum, a Hampton resident (Hampton is twelve miles northwest of Henderson):

"I was in the storm at Hampton in Hamilton County. The snow drifted the streets so that you could not see the buildings on either side. The Burlington Railroad ran only as far as Grand Island at that time. On account of the storm the railroad workers kept the snow plows on the main line from Lincoln to Denver. It took ten days to get the track cleared from Lincoln to Grand Island. I was a subscriber to the *Omaha Daily Bee* (at $10 a year) and the first mail train that got through brought me ten copies of the paper."

✳   ✳   ✳

*See Addenda for Chapter 7: "Stories of Helen and David Henderson and Their Neighborhood"

Lena

My name is Lena and I am eleven.
I am quiet, strong of body and will.
Father died when I was five from the
dreadful disease of smallpox.
I too had smallpox leaving me with a pocked face. I survived.
My mother, Wilhemine, had two more husbands
and lives near Milford. Of eleven children, three die.
I am the least favored child and I'm farmed out
as of last August to Woebbecke relatives near Seward.
My lunchpail and reader accompany me
to District No. 71 at Pleasant Dale.
Miss Stella Badger is the teacher; she is strict.
In school only English is spoken. I speak very little English.
January twelve, eighteen eighty-eight,
the blizzard comes with snow and sudden wind and cold.
A neighbor living near school comes for the schoolchildren
and teacher. "Come to my house," he said.
An older boy, Anton Blake, and I insist
that we will walk home instead.
We do not agree on the best route, whether road or ravine.
Anton goes his way and I go mine.
Halfway home I know I am lost; I'm lost in the storm.
Going this way and then that way, I wear myself out.
I fall asleep on the hillside,
drifting in and out of consciousness all night.
At dawn, Mr. Woebbecke finds me
and takes me, my lunchpail, and reader home.
My frozen right foot is amputated above the ankle. I survived.
I am nursed back to health by a kind woman in Milford.
She takes me in.
Schoolchildren's coins pay for my doctor bills
and my wooden foot.
I walk again. I go to school. I learn English.
I graduate. I marry.

Heartbreaking stories abound of teachers and schoolchildren challenged by the blizzard of January 1888. Some children experienced frostbite. All, whether remaining at the schoolhouse or en route home, shared feelings of an empty stomach. Others owed their lives to a teacher whose quick actions and wise decisions saved them. Still, a broad spectrum of variables determined the outcome. The following is an account of a girl living east of Henderson who went to school that day.

Lena's Story

I am Lena Schlesselmer Woebbecke. My father, Johann Friedrich Schlesselmer, died of smallpox when I was five years old. I also had smallpox, which badly scarred my face. I've always felt awkward when people stare at me. My mother, Wilhemine Schlesselmer, told me my pockmarks will keep suitors away and I will never marry. So mostly I keep to myself and I don't talk much. Mother married twice more. Many children were born into the household – eleven in all, with eight surviving. I am my stepfather's least favorite child.

In August 1887, my mother "farmed" me out to the Woebbecke relatives, Wilhelm and Catherina, who, like her, came from Herkensen, Germany. I moved from a farm near Milford, Nebraska, to the hilly land south of Seward. Life there was an improvement, and I have used Woebbecke for my last name ever since. The Woebbeckes' three little children left me alone except when I was asked to mind them. My job at the Woebbeckes was to help with chores and do outside work such as milk, herd cows, and carry water. This suited me just fine! I have a physique like a worker – I'm both sturdy and strong.

When the fall harvest was over, I was sent to school. I walked the half-mile shortcut through the ravines to District No. 71 at Pleasant Dale. All the pupils in my direction from the school liked the shortcut of the "Bohemian Alps" – that's what we called the ravines and irregular countryside. Our neighborhood consisted of people who had Czech and German backgrounds. Every school day I carried my lunchpail and reader. I stayed home from school whenever it snowed – even a little bit – because the ravines filled up with snow two to three times my height. Because of the deep ravines, with all the brush and the hill beyond, I couldn't see the hip-roofed school from the house. When going to the German Lutheran Church, we went the opposite direction.

My teacher, Stella Badger, was strict and allowed only English. No one spoke German in school. Whenever she wanted me to do something that didn't make sense to me or I didn't want to do, I looked down or past her. I told her – in my head, in German – what I thought of her and shut off whatever she was saying. She couldn't make me think or speak in English! To her, I was a stubborn and a quiet person. And she couldn't make me do something I didn't want to do!

January 12, 1888, changed my mind about not listening to my teacher. Miss Badger always said, for safety reasons, to use the straight roads going to and from school. I wish I had listened to her.

Following the afternoon recess that day, the schoolhouse got really dark. The teacher told us to stay at our desks and that we had enough fuel to last until the storm would pass. Then we heard stomping in the cloakroom. A farmer living nearby opened the door and said he wanted to take his children home. He was covered in snow. After visiting with Miss Badger about the weather, they decided all of us would go to the neighbor's home. All of the children, except for one older boy named, Anton Blake, Miss Badger, and I lived in the same direction as the snow-covered man. When it came time to go with him, I wasn't so sure about doing that. The farmer told the teacher we had to go immediately.

I wondered how the Woebbeckes would know where I was. I decided I wasn't about to go to another house! I'd walk home! Anton offered to stay and walk with me. The teacher reluctantly said the two of us could go. But Anton and I argued, shouting into the wind and using hand gestures, because we couldn't agree on which route to take. Anton wanted to walk along the road and I'd hear nothing of it. I started to walk across the stubble field toward the ravine like I always did. He hollered at me, but I didn't pay any attention to him and we parted ways.

About halfway home, I stopped. Something wasn't right. I was lost. At least I had my lunchpail and reader that the Woebbeckes insisted I bring home every night. I remembered Miss Badger had said there was plenty of coal at the school so I turned around to go back. I knew I was getting closer to the school, but suddenly I felt so tired and cold, and then everything went blank.

When I woke up, I thought I saw smoke rising from our chimney so I started for home again. Even if Miss Badger was right about taking the road instead of the shortcut, I would take the path through the ravine, and I kept going. But I didn't get far and collapsed again. My eyelids were hard to keep open because of the ice and snow and I was so cold. But I managed to drag myself down the hill. During the night, I laid on the side of the hill and drifted in and out of consciousness.

When dawn came and it was light enough to see, Mr. Woebbecke came looking for me. He had come to the school the previous afternoon, but no one was there.

When he spotted me on the other side of the ravine, he called my name. I heard him, but I had no voice to give a response. My eyes were mostly frozen shut. I got up on my knees, but I couldn't get up any further. I held up my lunch pail and reader to show that I remembered to bring them home. I was so glad to see Mr. Woebbecke. I put my arms around his neck as he lifted me off the ground and clung to him tightly. I couldn't speak, even in German, to tell him that I was glad to see him. He carried me back to the house. They took off my wet clothes and put me to bed. I went blank again.

George Burkett, the Superintendent of Public Institutions for Seward County, took an interest in my welfare. I needed medical attention and Mr. Burkett contacted Dr. G.W. Brandon, the Woebbeckes' family doctor from Milford. Dr. Brandon said that I had extreme frostbite and an advanced stage of gangrene in my right foot. They had to amputate it above the ankle.

The Woebbecke family was quite poor and couldn't pay the medical expenses. Since I was a student under Mr. Burkett's jurisdiction, he started a fund on my behalf. Mr. Burkett, with the Woebbeckes' blessing, was appointed guardian and trustee of the fund. Students across the state brought pennies, nickels, and dimes to school to help blizzard victims like me with medical expenses. Dr. Brandon knew of a German woman in Milford who would care for me. That summer, I received a new wooden foot, which helped me walk again.

In fall, when it was time to start school, Mr. Burkett moved me to Lincoln, where I was enrolled in the C Street School. My English improved immensely and I actually enjoyed attending public school. When Mr. Burkett moved me to Lincoln, he invested $3,750 for me at 8 percent interest. I owe much to Mr. Burkett for looking after me and my education. Perhaps one day I can show my appreciation to all who have helped me by helping others with their needs. I'd like that.

❄ ❄ ❄

After graduation, Lena entered Union College, a Seventh-Day Adventist school. On her seventeenth birthday, she received the benefits of the invested money, now totaling $4,939.46. With that money, she bought a thank-you gift for Mr. Burkett and purchased a farm near Milford. She returned home to the community where she was born and to the place that nurtured her to health following the blizzard. It was also an opportunity for Lena to mend the relationship with her mother.

Lena was twenty-four when she married George Schopp, but she died less than two years later, at age twenty-five. One can only surmise the cause of death: childbirth, lingering complications from the amputation, disease, accident. She was buried in her wedding dress and laid to rest at the Immanuel Lutheran Church cemetery. Coincidentally, Lena's mother, Wilhemine Dorgeloh, died a few days later at fifty-two. She was laid to rest beside the daughter she had abandoned fourteen years earlier, but with whom she had made peace.

*See Addenda for Chapter Seven: History and Development of the Word "Blizzard" in the Nineteenth Century

RECIPE
SNOW ICE CREAM BLIZZARD
Serves 4

UTENSILS
    Bowl, medium size, for eggs, vanilla, salt, sugar, and milk/cream
    Spoon to mix
    Pan, large size, for clean snow

INGREDIENTS
    Eggs 2
    Vanilla 1 T.
    Salt 1/8 t.
    Sugar 1/2 cup
    Milk (part cream) 1/2 cup
    Snow

METHOD
    Beat eggs.
    Mix in vanilla, salt, sugar, and milk/cream.
    Stir snow into mixture to desired consistency.
    Serve immediately.

ADD
    Stir in crushed candy or small pieces of a candy bar for a
        "Blizzard."

OPTION
    Replace sugar and milk/cream with 1 can of sweetened condensed
        milk.

Gertrune

My name is Gertrune Jane, Gertie for short.
I am eight years old
and live one mile from school with my family –
mother, Justina Gertrune; father, Martin Emil;
and little brother, Franklin Emil, who is five.
I haven't been tardy or absent from school.
School is in Newton Township, one mile east of
Spencer Road on First Street and one mile south.
My teacher, Miss Peomelia D. Walton,
teaches grades one through eight at
Kellas School District No. 35.
I learn reading, writing, and arithmetic
and listen to older students recite lessons in
geography and United States history.
During the January twelve, eighteen eighty-eight blizzard,
Miss Walton shouts to the snow plastered windows
a poem by William Shakespeare,
"Blow, Blow, Thou Winter Wind."
I had never heard Miss Walton talk so loud.
We learned the refrain before Christmas
and everyone sang the refrain loud, very loud.
Pupils then listened to the poem "Old Winter"
by Thomas Noel.
I liked the last line when students together shouted,
"We'll keep old winter out!"
Then
my father came for me. Blankets were stacked
in the wheat wagon, enough to cover all.
First, we took teacher and pupils across the road
to the Kellas family
and then my father took me home to mine.
I love my very own family, my school family,
and my neighborhood family.

CHAPTER EIGHT

Gertrune from Newton

Located in Kansas of the United States of America

Date: January 12, 1888
High: 32 F. (0 C.)
Low: 10 F. (-11 C.)
Wind: South turning North

Justina Gertrune Phinney frantically scurries, looking for a towel, and sputters to her daughter, "Gertie, help me by taking the bacon, eggs, and biscuits to the table while I clean up Frankie's spilled milk."

Eight-year-old Gertrune Jane, Gertie for short, accustomed to being a helper, carries the food to the table. Five-year-old Franklin Emil, sitting at the breakfast table, tipped his glass of milk when he energetically waved to his father, Martin Emil Phinney, who was coming in after chores. Frankie has been waiting patiently at the table for his father so breakfast could begin. With the spill cleaned up, the morning meal gets underway.

It's Thursday morning, January 12, 1888.

"What is happening in school today, Gertie?" Martin asks. "Are you expecting the county superintendent to visit again this morning?"

"The third through eighth graders are going to learn a new kind of poem this afternoon during language class. When they finish their writing project, the older students will help the younger," Gertie says. "It has something to do with Kansas, and we are to think about everything that is special about Kansas because we became a state in 1861."

"I doubt the county school superintendent will visit us again, since he visited on Monday."

Gertie smiles as she recalls how she told her family about their visitor at school Monday.

"The older students take turns answering the door, whenever there is a knock. Miss Walton, our teacher, nodded to Grant Shutt, who was seated closest to the door, to let the visitor inside. When he opened the door, Grant's face turned white. I thought he would faint. There stood Mr. Samuel Danner, the county superintendent. You could hear the whispers all around the classroom, 'It's the county superintendent.'"

"Miss Walton smiled as she got up from behind the teacher's desk. Then she put her index finger on her lips to quiet us and reached for the back of the empty chair beside her own chair. That's the chair she uses when she helps a student. She carried the chair to the back of the room, just like this happens every day. She invited our guest to be comfortable."

"Miss Walton later told us that she is an officer of the Harvey County Education Association, so she knows the county superintendent and that he was not a stranger. We all knew it was an important visit, and we did our best to make a good impression. Our class sessions went on."

"We were all glad the school was clean and tidy. On Friday, before the noon break was over, the older students had spread sweeping compound – sawdust mixed with oil – on the floor. We walked all over it, and it collected all the dust and dirt from the week. After sweeping, we had a shiny clean floor. This was our last duty before we were dismissed. There seemed to be a job for all the older children while the younger ones colored at their desks. Every Friday, it's supposed to be a picture of a different bird. Some of us wiped the chalkboard and others made sure the slates were collected and stacked. We cleaned our desks inside and out. One student from each row was the desk inspector to make sure items in the desks were arranged neatly. I think the county superintendent was impressed that we were all so well-behaved and everything was tidy."

Martin rouses Gertie from her thoughts and makes an offer she can't turn down.

"Gertie, hurry and pack your lunch in the syrup pail if you want to catch a ride to school and get there early. After all, you haven't been tardy or absent all year, plus it will save you the time of walking one mile. I'm going to help Henry Kellas with a project in his barn this morning. Since he lives right across the road from the school, maybe you want us to be your visitors today," Martin teased.

Gertie raises her freckled nose up a notch, lowers her eyes, squints, and says, "But we have only one extra chair." They both laugh.

Many pupils in 1888 carried their lunch in a syrup pail with a handle. Lunch often was rye bread smeared with bacon grease and accompanied by breakfast leftovers. The oldest children's task in the morning – if there was no well at the school – was to go to the nearest neighbor to fill a cream can or bucket with water and bring it back to the school. It was normal to drink from a common cup. Water was poured into a large crock and dipped out with a dipper into a cup used by all the students. Sometimes only a water pail with a dipper was available.

The Kellas District No. 35 schoolhouse was built in 1873. As students grew and more children were born, a fourteen-by-sixteen-foot addition was built to accommodate the older children. This expansion, anticipated by the original builders, had a centrally located door on the righthand side of the building, where there was only one window while the parallel wall had three. The inside of the original schoolroom had nine coat hooks on either side of the front door with a shelf above the hooks for the lunch pails. Below the windows, and continuing below the chalkboard at the front of the room, was vertical, dark-brown, wainscoting.

In the front of the room, behind the teacher's desk and above the chalkboard, were pictures of George Washington and Abraham Lincoln. A flag holder with a Kansas flag was between the pictures.

Maps were stored in an enclosed wall cabinet to the right of the teacher's desk. Along the wall to the left of the teacher's desk was a cupboard for extra books and supplies like slates and chalk. There were two chairs behind the teacher's desk and the recitation bench was in front of it. The students sat on that bench when called to the front to demonstrate their knowledge.

School began at 9 a.m., with a 15-minute opening that usually included singing. Then students in each grade recited their lessons in turn. Texts such as *Raub's Readers First Through Fifth Grades* were used for the lower grades. A 15-minute break at 10:30 for recess was followed by math classes, using *Walton's Arithmetic Curriculum*, until noon. The school board members and the teacher, Miss Peomelia D. Walton, decided on the arithmetic syllabus for the students. Teachers used their discretion on how to include the arts and often enriched the standard subjects with them.

Everyone took an hour at noon to eat lunch and then continued the game started at morning recess. The bell rang at 1 p.m., for school to resume. The teacher usually read for 15 minutes from a novel, to be continued the following day. Lessons from *Specimen Penmanship*, *Harvey's Grammar*, *Barnes' Brief United States History*, or *Guygots' Geography* continued in the afternoon, with a fifteen-minute recess break at 2:30. School was dismissed at 4.

Gertie likes to listen to the older students recite their lessons. It is learning without knowing that one is learning. She finds the lessons to be very interesting. It's like having a daily story-time.

While the students are in class this Thursday morning, Martin E. Phinney and Henry Kellas sit down on the nail kegs in Henry's barn across the road from the Kellas School. Henry, just back from Newton with supplies, also brought the morning newspaper, *The Newton Daily Republican*. Both men are eager to check the weather for the day on the front page before beginning their project. The January 12, 1888 issue has a 1 a.m., weather forecast from Washington, D.C. The prediction is for fair weather, followed by snow. The brisk and slight southerly winds will diminish in force and become westerly with warmer followed by colder weather, the paper forecasts.

As the men work, they chat about their crops and reminisce. They talk about the difference the Turkey red hard winter wheat has made in their farming and how that has helped ensure there is enough income to take care of the school building across the road. Henry asks Martin if he remembers how the winter wheat got to Kansas.

Martin, with a bent for history, launches into how he remembers the story.

"German immigrants from South Russia brought Turkey red hard winter wheat to Kansas and this really made the difference. One young man in particular, Bernhard Warkentin Jr., changed agriculture for us. He and three other young men of sufficient means traveled independently and arrived in the United States June 5, 1872. They looked for land similar to that of the 'breadbasket' in Russia. Bernhard liked Kansas. His father, Bernhard Aron Warkentin Sr., had introduced Turkey red hard winter wheat to southern Russia twelve years earlier, in 1860. Like father, like son!"

Henry wants to know more about the kind of education Warkentin had.

Martin elaborates. "Bernhard attended McKendrie College at Lebanon, Illinois. He had graduated from a business school in Russia, but he wanted to keep on improving his knowledge. Bernhard Jr. had a vision to make Kansas the 'Breadbasket of America.'"

Henry muses, "Newton has become quite a community since both of our families arrived here from Europe in 1871. Do you know how Newton got its start?"

Martin continues the history lesson. "Newton was named after Newton, Massachusetts, the hometown of Santa Fe Railroad stockholders. Newton's townsite was laid out August 24, 1870, to accommodate the Santa Fe Railroad, the southernmost railroad terminal. Within six months, settlers arrived. By July, Newton was platted. The first passenger train arrived July 17, 1871. With settlers arriving, the Newton community became more populated, and public schools were built. Henry, do you remember the first school board meeting we had in this district?" asks Martin.

"I remember that well," Henry answers. "Farmers living southeast of Newton met September 15, 1873, to propose a bond for $600 to build a school. Since Kansas had passed a law in 1861 that women could vote in school district elections, several women came and voted to build a school. Our wives were so proud to sign in. Three women – J.G. Phinney, S. Hatfield, and A. Kellas – were among the eighteen citizens who cast their votes for building a school. With 100 percent support, a location was approved. The school was built one mile east of Spencer Road on First Street and one mile south. Since we owned the land across the road from the school, they named it the Kellas School. This was the 35th school in Harvey County to be organized and registered, hence the name, District No. 35."

It's almost noon when Martin finishes helping Henry with his project. Driving west to his farm, he notices a peculiar dense haze on the horizon. Arriving home, he has just enough time to check his livestock before joining Justina and Frankie for the noon meal. Before the meal was completed, Frankie is excited to see snow is falling and wants to go outside. Just as forecast, the snow followed the warm weather. Big flakes come down and soon develop into a heavy snowfall. It snows into the afternoon.

Even bigger changes in weather come later that afternoon. Around 3 p.m., the wind turns suddenly from the south to the north. Never have Martin and Justina experienced such an abrupt change in weather. The temperature drops and the wind starts blowing stronger and stronger. The weather forecast in the paper didn't say anything about high wind. This certainly isn't the "slight southerly winds that will diminish in force" described in the morning paper, Martin thinks. The wind is blowing very hard and the temperature continues to drop rapidly. Justina frantically looks out the window and sees Martin hitching the wheat wagon to the horse. She knows that he is planning to go to the school. Then, as she watches him come towards the house, she acts on instinct. Justina knows exactly what she needs to do.

She goes to the trunk, set to the side of the main room and hurriedly lifts the lid. Justina loads her arms with all the extra blankets stored there and meets Martin at the door.

"Here, Martin, put these under the tarp to keep dry. And bring back our little Gertie!"

No sooner are the blankets fastened under the tarp than Martin is off to the schoolhouse. The wind blows with an intensity he has never experienced. The weather forecast did say there would be colder weather, but this cold? It feels especially cold in this wind.

Back at school, following the afternoon recess, Miss Walton begins the writing class for the intermediate and older pupils. One day a week it is penmanship. On another day, it could be writing a poem to memorize. She gives instructions and explains today's assignment.

"Acrostic is a poem in which a word is read downward. Together we'll describe Kansas with something that begins with each letter. Yesterday, I asked you to think about what is special about Kansas. Let's work on this acrostic together.

K ansa Indians are people of the south wind who lived long ago in farming villages by Kansas rivers.

A rkansas River is the longest river in Kansas and flows into the Missouri River.

N icodemus is a town settled by freed slaves in 1876 by Benjamin "Pap" Singleton, a carpenter.

S unflowers grow wild in Kansas. The state flower is the common sunflower.

A bilene is along the cattle trail where cowboys drove cattle to ship by rail until the early 1870s.

S oddy is a home – made from thick chunks of grassy sod cut from the earth and used like bricks.

"Now that we have finished the acrostic of Kansas, you may write your name vertically. Then write about yourself, beginning with the letters on the left-hand side. Write about who you are in a word, phrase, or sentence. Use as many words as you like."

Then, while students busily write an acrostic of their name, the weather suddenly changes. Miss Walton nervously peers out the window, aware of the increasingly howling wind and the relentless snow and debris smashing against the windows. Children stop and sit wide-eyed at their desks and look at her with furrowed foreheads. The darkening room and roaring wind are disconcerting. She quickly calms the children with a distraction.

Placing her hands on her hips, and with a fierce expression on her face, Miss Walton lashes out at the snow-pasted window and begins reciting "Blow, Blow, Thou Winter Wind" by William Shakespeare. Having learned the refrain before Christmas, the students know exactly when to come in. Miss Walton, with a determination her students have never encountered before, begins in a loud voice:

> *Blow, blow, thou winter wind,*
> *Thou art not so unkind*
> *As Man's ingratitude;*
> *Thy tooth is not so keen,*
> *Because thou art not seen,*
> *Although thy breath be rude.*

She motions to the students to chime in, and at the top of their lungs, they sing:

> *Heigh-ho! Sing heigh-ho! Unto the green holly;*
> *Most friendship is feigning, most loving mere folly:*
> *Then, heigh-ho, the holly!*
> *This life is most jolly!*

The teacher points to herself and continues:

> *Freeze, freeze, thou bitter sky,*
> *Thou dost not bite so nigh*
> *As benefits forgot:*
> *Though thou the waters warp,*
> *Thy sting is not so sharp*
> *As friend remembered not.*

Miss Walton directs with a beat the refrain, inviting full participation:

> *Heigh-ho! Sing heigh-ho! Unto the green holly;*
> *Most friendship is feigning, most loving mere folly:*
> *Then, heigh-ho, the holly!*
> *This life is most jolly!*

Gertie raises her hand and asks, "Why don't I feel jolly?"

Miss Walton smiles and motions to the children to gather around her. She navigates her clutch closer to the potbelly stove to the right of her desk. As she stoops to feed the stove some coal from the coal bucket, her eyes meet Gertie's. "Winter is feeling out of sorts today and it can make people feel anxious and sad," Miss Walton tells her.

Gertie looks intently at her teacher and pleads in her lisping voice, "Please, Miss Walton, say a poem to help us feel better. Please, Miss Walton?"

Miss Walton takes stock of the situation, with both short-term and long-term consequences flitting through her mind, smiles at Gertie and all her students, and launches into "Old Winter" by Thomas Noel.

> Old Winter sad, in snowy clad,
>   is making a doleful din;
> But let him howl till he crack his jowl,
>   We will not let him in.
> Ay, let him lift from the billowy drift
>   His hoary, haggard form,
> And scowling stand, with his wrinkled hand
>   Outstretching to the storm.
> And let his weird and sleety beard
>   Stream loose upon the blast,
> And, rustling, chime to the tinkling rime
>   From his bald head falling fast.
> Let his baleful breath shed blight and death
>   On herb and flower and tree;
> And brooks and ponds in crystal bonds
>   Bind fast, but what care we?
> Let him push at the door, – in the chimney roar,
>   And rattle the window-pane;
> Let him in at us spy with his icicle eye,
>   But he shall not entrance gain.
> Let him gnaw, forsooth, with his freezing tooth,
>   On our roof-tiles, till he tire;
> But we care not a whit, as we jovial sit
>   Before our blazing fire.
> Come, lads, let's sing, till the rafters ring;
>   Come push the can about; –
> From our snug fire-side this Christmas-tide
>   We'll keep old Winter out.

"Yeah!" howl the students applauding spontaneously. The children echo in unison the last line, "We'll keep old Winter out."

Suddenly, at that very moment, they hear a clumping sound outside and the door to the classroom bursts open.

It's Martin, Gertie's father.

Recognizing him as he removes the scarf from around his head, Gertie gets up and runs to her father, saying, "Now I feel jolly!"

Following the brief father-and-daughter reunion, Miss Walton and Martin, who has come a mile from his home, make plans for what will happen next with the fifteen students in attendance. Altogether, four inches of snow has already accumulated that day. But it's the plummeting cold temperatures and high winds that make it unsafe to be out in the swirling snow.

Three options surface.

One: Stay at the school and wait for parents to come. The problem is that they have no food, no adequate clothing, and fuel is limited. Plus, there is no guarantee parents will arrive before morning.

Two: Martin will take all the children to their respective homes. But exposure to the elements is risky, even with the blankets that have been brought from the Phinney home.

Three: Go to the Kellas family across the road, where food and warmth will be provided.

The two adults decide the best option is to transport all the students across the road to the Kellas family. The children bundle up under the blankets and prepare for the wintry ride. They arrive safely. The students and the teacher are sheltered, safe, and warm that night. Mr. Phinney then takes Gertie home to her very own family.

❄   ❄   ❄

In the wake of the blizzard, Kansans help the destitute beyond their community to the far reaches of the state by collecting and distributing provisions of food and clothing. A train left Wichita, January 15, 1888, carrying precious cargo of food and clothing to Ashland in Clark County north of the Oklahoma border. It is estimated that 3,000 people in Clark County were in need, having suffered from the cold for several weeks already. In reality, Kansans as a whole were ill-prepared for the cold weather.

❄   ❄   ❄

*See Addenda for Chapter Eight: "More Survival Stories of Kansas Students and Teachers During the January 12, 1888 Blizzard"; "Bernhard Warkentin Jr. and the Economics of Turkey Red Winter Wheat"; "Schools"

RECIPE
ROASTED SUNFLOWER SEEDS

Bake at 325° for 25-30 minutes.

UTENSILS

Saucepan, 3-quart size
Colander or strainer
Cookie sheet or large shallow pan

INGREDIENTS

Sunflower seeds (unshelled) 2 cups
Water 2 quarts
Salt 1/4 to 1/2 cup

METHOD

Rinse unshelled sunflower seeds in a strainer and remove any plant or flowerhead matter.

Place fresh water, salt, and unshelled sunflower seeds in a saucepan.

Bring water to a boil, then turn down to simmer.

Simmer 1-1½ hours.

Strain water and seeds through colander (DO NOT RINSE).

Dry seeds on paper or cloth towel.

Preheat oven to 325°.

Spread seeds on a cookie sheet and bake 25-30 minutes.

Stir frequently.

Remove from oven when seeds are slightly brown and fragrant.

Edith

My name is Edith.
I am seven years old.
Reading is difficult; my ears become my book.
Mother tells stories; I observe; I ask questions; I listen.
Father manages cattle, mostly for Kansas ranchers
in the Cherokee Outlet of Indian Territory.
The Cherokee Tribal Council leases land
to the Cherokee Strip Livestock Association.
That is why we live here; my dad manages the association.
He is president.
Thursday, January twelve, eighteen eighty-eight,
by two in the afternoon, the temperature is in the upper forties,
one degree short of fifty.
There is snow by four and when the clock strikes bed-time
there is a low of twenty-six;
it snows and blows.
The next morning the temperature drops to nine degrees;
by Sunday it is thirteen below zero.
Father says, "Ranching is a gamble of sorts;
nature determines the outcome."
Cattle freeze, grass blades freeze,
ranchers in search of cattle freeze.
I listen to conversation and hear that
thin-skinned cattle are no match for this weather.
Father says, "Next time, next season, next herd;
it will be better.
We'll have better weather,
with tougher cattle, stronger corrals,
and a higher price when we sell.
Next year will be better."
I whisper an echo – next year will be better.

CHAPTER NINE

Edith from Enid

Located in the Cherokee Outlet of Indian Territory
Later (1890) Oklahoma Territory
and then much later (1907) the state of Oklahoma

January 12, 1888
High: 49 F. (9 C.)
Low: 26 F. (-4 C.)
Wind: NW

When the January 12, 1888 weather system reaches Indian Territory at 2 p.m., the temperature begins to drop from the day's balmy high of 49 degrees. By 4 p.m., rain turns to snow as the temperature continues to fall.

The Naylor family, Harry, Mary, and seven-year-old Edith, is unprepared for the sudden change in weather. Even though it is getting colder, they can't help but notice the change of scenery. The family marvels at the unusual presentation of moisture. They are amazed at the beauty of the heavy, free-falling flakes of snow streaming down in an unending vertical flow. That is something one doesn't see too often in this sixty-mile-wide and 225-mile-long parcel of land. This grassy patch stretches along the Kansas border and is known as the Cherokee Outlet. It is leased by the Cherokee Nation to the Cherokee Strip Livestock Association for five years at $100,000 each year.

Harry's job as president and manager of this livestock association involves care of the cattle owned by members of the association, mostly cattlemen from Kansas. Before the 1883-1888 five-year lease, the Kansas ranchers independently paid the Cherokee Nation an agreed-upon sum. Even ranchers passing through the Outlet on their way to Abilene to ship cattle were expected to pay ten cents a head to the Cherokee. That system was quite chaotic and random for the Cherokee as there was no designated place to enter and exit the Outlet. So creating the leasing arrangement was a win-win.

Hoping the weather will change soon, Harry fidgets. He feels helpless, knowing he can't protect the association's cattle from the snow and cold. Snow continues to fall and, as the temperature keeps dropping, the northwest wind picks up. The Naylor family, with this unexpected family time, keeps warm and occupied in conversation while snacking between meals.

Edith, delighted to have her father's attention, brings him her shallow treasure box to admire. Inside are small containers of berries, sticks, pieces of broken glass separated by color, crushed peanut shells, and more. She uses these items to make pictures. She even sells some at the local Mercantile and Harness Shop. Cowboys traveling through buy them as gifts for their families back home. As items are sold from the shelves, Edith replaces them with new creations.

"Father, when my friend, Gloria, and I play together, we make our own pictures and sometimes trade from our collection of things. Do you sometimes make a trade with others?"

Harry, amused with Edith's question, hugs her and smiles.

"The trading I do is usually for money, like selling cattle. Our livestock association pays the Cherokee Tribal Council to use the Cherokee Outlet. I guess that's a trade, but it is for five years at a time. When you sell one of your pictures for money, that is a trade too."

Edith is quite pleased with herself. She wonders about a phrase she has heard used often. Looking intently at her father, Edith asks, "Why is this called a Cherokee Outlet?"

"The Cherokee Outlet gets its name because the Cherokee Nation owns it. The word 'outlet' describes the land as a way out of the property, a passageway. The Cherokee live near the northeastern part of Indian Territory, south of the Kansas border. Buffalo roam beyond the western border of the Outlet's grassy area. Going 'out' of the Outlet to another region to hunt buffalo or 'out' of the Outlet north to Kansas with a herd of cattle describes how one makes a passageway from one piece of land to another."

"From where did the Cherokee come?" Edith wants to know.

"My, oh my, aren't we full of questions. Why don't you and your mother first tell me what you did this morning, and then we'll get back to your Cherokee question, okay?"

Edith nods, and Mary appreciates the invitation to join the conversation. She explains a bit about their morning efforts at homeschooling.

"It was an absolutely gorgeous morning, and since I had some errands to run at the mercantile, Edith and I made a morning walk of it. As we walked, I asked her to read signs above the places of business or in the store windows."

Edith, wanting to display both her progress and frustration in learning words, explains how the lesson works.

"Mother would say, 'What is this word, Edith?' as she pointed to the signs. Sometimes I guessed because the letter sounds don't always make sense to me. I figure out what they sell in the store and what I have heard others talk about. And then I guess with some hints from the letters in the word. It works, but I don't always read it correctly."

"And then we stopped to see the new sign outside our town, remember, Edith?" said Mary.

The sign, recently erected at the edge of their unincorporated town, has the letters 'ENID' carved into a piece of wood and nailed to a post.

"Oh yes," Edith recalls. "Since I have learned the sounds of the alphabet, I made the sounds of the letters, D-I-N-E, 'dine.' But Mother said it was 'Enid' so I must have started from the wrong end of the word. It is so hard for me to turn things around before I say them."

Edith struggles as she learns to read. It takes so much concentration, effort, and time for her to figure out words. It is frustrating. Her mother has discovered that Edith learns most easily by observation, asking questions, and listening. She decides her daughter isn't ready to learn at school.

But she marvels at how Edith can draw and make beautiful pictures from seemingly nothing. In her spare time, when not helping her mother with housework, Edith sits in her happy place and creates beautiful pictures and wall hangings.

Edith has a vivid imagination. She tells her father something else about their experience when she and her mother went to see the new "Enid" sign that morning. "When we walked to the edge of town, I wondered if, by chance, we could see you. Father, I thought maybe we would see you feeding hay to the cattle. I imagined I could see the cattle walking along the cow path to the stream that runs into the Cimarron River. Perhaps it was mostly imagination, but I thought I could actually see the cattle walking single file."

Mary continues, recalling their purchase at the mercantile.

"Remember, after that we stopped by the mercantile to purchase those raw Spanish peanuts that grow so well in central and southern Indian Territory. While the two of you were admiring treasure box items and visiting about the Cherokee Outlet, I cleaned the pots and pans that were used to make these burnt sugar peanuts to snack on."

Making herself comfortable near the fire, Mary shares the peanut snack and gives an extra blanket to Harry and Edith. These colorful blankets, placed around the room for decoration, were bought or traded in the last five years. They wrap a blanket around their shoulders to help take the chill out of the air. It is getting colder outside and the roar of the wind sounds ferocious. The pinging of dirt and ice pelting against the window is noisy.

"Edith, you asked about where the Cherokee came from," Mary says. "This would be a good time to talk about that."

"Much of Oklahoma in the 1800s was a huge Indian reservation," she explained. "In fact, two Choctaw Indian words were combined to form Oklahoma: *okla* means people and *homa* means red."

In 1830, President Andrew Jackson signed the Indian Removal Act of 1830. That law forced five Indian Nations from the southeastern part of the United States to walk to the Indian Territory. It was a very sad procession known as the Trail of Tears. Can you imagine being forced to walk more than 2,000 miles across nine states? It took a long time – a very long time. Oh my, just think about the suffering they endured from hunger, starvation, sickness, and disease. The dead were buried along the way."

"Their route got even longer because they were forced to walk around towns and cities. City dwellers didn't want the illness near their homes and businesses. They didn't have adequate clothing. Imagine walking barefoot along the muddy and frozen trail, with your feet unprotected. Threads barely held their clothing together and provided little shielding against the heavy rain, snow, and freezing temperatures. This made for a difficult journey."

"Do you think they would have had weather like we are having this afternoon when they were forced to walk?" Edith asks, thinking about the poorly dressed travelers.

"Yes," answers Harry. "And it went on, day after day, day and night. Their feet got cut and bruised and sometimes frozen. They were so cold and hungry. It is little wonder they got sick and so many died."

Mary adds, "Sometimes they had to cross a river and that could be dangerous. Crossing a body of water by ferry was a wait-and-see situation. Local people were given first chance, and the forced travelers had to wait until the end of the day, not knowing if it would even happen. They huddled to wait with hardly any protection from the weather. More died while waiting to cross the river. And when they got their chance, the high price they had paid often left them penniless. Often the bare necessities they needed to stay alive had vanished. It's hard to imagine the hardship and difficulties they endured. It is little wonder that 4,000 of the more than 16,000 Cherokee died in that walk."

A sad-looking Edith said, "Why would anyone force them to leave their home? There must have been children my age on that trail."

"Yes," Mary says, "and mothers, fathers, and grandparents too."

Mary loves Edith's empathy. With a heavy heart, she continues her story. "It seems settlers from the eastern part of our country wanted to live on the land where the Cherokee, Chickasaw, Choctaw, Creek, and Seminole tribes lived. These tribes were primarily farmers and had a long history of governing themselves and caring for the earth. They eventually settled in Indian Territory."

"Did these farmers grow the Spanish peanuts we bought this morning?" asked Edith.

"It is possible that someone from the Chickasaw Nation harvested these peanuts, the ones we call raw Spanish peanuts," Mary says. "They call them Spanish peanuts because people came here from Spain searching for gold. They brought different seeds to America, and these peanuts grow really well in some of the soil here. And before you ask if the Spaniards found gold, the answer is no, they did not find gold in our part of America."

Edith smiles, amused at how well her mother knows what she was thinking. Looking at her father, she says, "Tell me more about the Cherokee Outlet where we are now living."

"The Outlet is a good place for cattle coming from Texas to rest before going further," he said. "It has many streams of water and lots of grass for them to eat. Enid is on the Chisholm Trail route, but about twenty years ago, this area became busy with cattle drives following the cattle trail to Abilene."

"Father, you told me we moved to Enid five years ago because of your new cattle job. You said that was for five years. We have lived here for five years. Does that mean we have to move away from here?"

"No, Edith, we won't move just yet," Harry says. "The Cherokee Tribal Council has leased the Cherokee Outlet to the association for another five years, so we'll be staying."

The family gathers around the table for a supper of stew and cornbread. Edith's curiosity continues.

"So, five Indian tribes traveled the Trail of Tears. We know the most about the Cherokee since they are our neighbors. Where do the other Indian tribes live?"

Harry, happy to have time with his family, enjoys the conversation. As the storm rages outside, he is increasingly worried about the cattle, but there is little he can do now. He'll wait until morning to check on the livestock. For now, he is safe and warm, and he wants to make the most of it, so the conversation continues.

"The four other Indian tribes live south and southwest of the Cherokee, also in separate nation groups," he explains. "They have their own government and decide how their own tribes should run their schools. At least they did this until the children were forced to live in a school away from home. The school was run by someone paid by the United States government. Other Indian tribes continue to roam the prairies, following the buffalo. The federal government has put pressure on Kansas Indian tribes to leave their land and move south to be near other Indians in Indian Territory."

"Let me guess," says Edith. "So settlers coming from the east will have a place to live?"

The parents both nod yes.

"I'm afraid that is how it is," Mary says.

At bedtime, the mercury has dropped to 26 degrees. By morning, the temperature plummets to 9 above, very cold and unusual weather.

The challenge of keeping warm is a very real problem for people in Indian Territory who don't own clothing for this kind of weather. Mary and Edith look for cloth and sacks to use with blankets and hides to create layers; Harry will need the extra warmth when he goes outside to check the cattle.

Despite the continuing bad weather the morning of January 13, after some hot coffee and leftover cornbread, Harry goes out to check on the cattle. The wind has quit blowing, but it is very cold.

The thin-skinned Texas Longhorn cattle are quite unaccustomed to the snow and cold. Riding across the Outlet, Harry sees more frozen cattle than he thought possible. "This should not be happening," he tells himself.

Harry forms a plan for what to do with all the dead cattle. After the storm settles, they will collect the carcasses, harvest the hides, and sell them to help pay the Cherokee Tribal Council lease.

By Sunday, January 15, the temperature is 13 degrees below zero. Unaccustomed to a 62-degree drop in temperature, Mary and Edith are using everything they can repurpose to keep warm. It is a challenge for all families and inhabitants of Indian Territory to keep warm. The cold is also hard on the grass and the animals.

The toll in cattle loss for the Cherokee Strip Livestock Association is devastating. Harry had not anticipated the extreme cold. The dead cattle translate to a major financial setback, and it will take time to rebuild the cattle herd. Perhaps next year, the weather will be more moderate. "Perhaps next year we'll invest in a tougher breed of cattle," he thinks. "Perhaps next year the corrals will be stronger. Perhaps next year the market will be at an all-time high. Next year will be better."

❊ ❊ ❊

When the five-year lease came up for renewal on January 1, 1888, the Cherokee Tribal Council put it up for bids, hoping for a better price. The Cherokee Strip Livestock Association leased the Outlet for another five years at an annual fee of $200,000 each year, an increase of $100,000. That increase, coupled with the cattle loss in the January 1888 blizzard, hit the association hard. It was a struggle.

By 1888, there were more than one hundred members in the association. Members divided their responsibilities and built fences, corrals, and ranch houses, and collected fees from ranchers driving their cattle through the Outlet. Many association families lived in the Cherokee Outlet. Business opportunities began to arise in the growing town of Enid and businesses multiplied in the years that followed.

❊ ❊ ❊

*See Addenda for Chapter Nine: "Education in Indian Territory"

❊ ❊ ❊

RECIPE
BURNT SUGAR PEANUTS
Bake at 300° for 45 minutes.

UTENSILS
Saucepan
Cookie sheet with a lip
Scraper

INGREDIENTS
Water 1/2 cup
Sugar 1 cup
Butter flavor 1/2 t.
Maple flavor 1/2 t.
Salt 1/2 t.
Peanuts (raw) 3 cups

METHOD
Bring the above ingredients EXCEPT RAW PEANUTS to boil.
Add raw peanuts.
Boil 10 minutes.
Put mixture on HEAVILY greased cookie sheet.
Bake 45 minutes at 300°.
Cool.
Break apart.

Austin

My name is Austin.
I am twenty years old and attend University,
Texas University at Austin,
where I study Agricultural Economics.
My parents, David and Martha,
work at the church and manage the shelter respectively.
The shelter is called the Sharing Table.
Community people bring food and clothing for the needy.
My siblings, Sarah, who is eighteen, Jonah, who is sixteen,
Ruth, who is fourteen, and I,
after homework, help out at the shelter.
The Prairie Blizzard of January twelve, eighteen eighty-eight
with its cold icy needles, snow, and wind
arrives in Austin, Texas, Saturday, January fourteen.
Rain turns to snow.
Temperature falls suddenly
from seventy degrees to twenty-six in two hours.
Strong winds blow from the north.
"Norther"
the southerners call it.
The shelter is a net of safety
for the hungry and cold, like Thomas,
the thinly clad man.

CHAPTER TEN

Austin from Austin

Located in Texas of the United States of America

January 14, 1888
High: 70 F. (20 C.)
Low: 16 F. (-9 C.)
Wind: N

W alking the three blocks from his home to the Christian Church of Austin, Reverend David Langly – with sermon notes in his pocket – leaves before the family awakens. Practicing his sermon to an invisible congregation is his Saturday morning routine.

Martha, David's wife, manages the Sharing Table, a shelter attached to the church. Community people drop off food and clothes to be shared with anyone in need. Noticing the warm and sunny day as she rises on January 14, 1888, Martha decides, on impulse, to air out the bedding on the clothesline in their back yard. She enlists the help of her children – Austin, twenty; Sarah, eighteen; Jonah, sixteen; and Ruth, fourteen. After they have draped their blankets over the clothesline on this unbelievably gorgeous day, their Saturday morning chores begin.

Martha instructs: "Sarah, this is your week to bake bread. We have just enough bread tins to fill the oven with one recipe. Mix a double batch of bread dough today, and we'll make 'knee patches' with half of the dough and have them for our noon meal."

"Your brothers, after they finish their jobs, will take a piece of dough and stretch it over their bare knees until the dough is thin. Then let the patches rise on the floured table a bit and Ruth, who is your helper and the one cleaning in the kitchen today, can help with the deep-fat frying. We'll take what is left over from the noon meal to the Sharing Table this afternoon when we go for the weekly cleaning. We'll put the extra patches into the discarded pillowcase from the rag drawer."

The Langlys are descendants of one of the 300 colony families brought by Stephen Fuller Austin to Texas in 1823. The colonists came from the United States of America while Texas was governed by Spain. Austin attends Texas University at Austin, studying agricultural economics. His siblings go to Austin High School, a public school established in 1881. Austin's heart is with the people of this Texas city. There are so many needs locally, which helped him to decide on his major. The university is known for its research, and he wants to learn about growing the best crops for the right soil.

"Austin," says his mother, "it is your turn this week to get the groceries from the corner store. Make your last stop at the meat market for sausage links and cheese. The sausage will be for the noon meal and the cheese for Sunday. Here is the list and the money."

Preparing ahead of time for the Sunday noon meal is in keeping with making Sunday more restful at the Langly home. Jonah, knowing it is his turn to do a thorough cleaning of the parlor and dining room, begins by shaking and beating the rugs. Everyone sweeps and dusts their own bedrooms. The boys take turns with the jobs for their shared bedroom, and the girls do the same for theirs. Their father prides himself in the weekly routine of tidying the front porch and yard. He also engages friends and neighbors in conversation as they walk by. Martha busies herself with cleaning the master bedroom and cooking ahead for the evening meal and anything else needed for Sunday.

Everyone enjoys the noon meal. The house is tidy, sun-drenched bedding is back on the beds, and the family prepares to leave for the Sharing Table. Austin slings the pillowcase full of knee patches over his shoulder.

"You look like St. Nick," teases Jonah.

Suddenly, the wind shifts to the north. Martha looks toward the sky, sensing not all is well.

"Wait for me," she instructs.

Martha goes back into the house to find another pillowcase in the rag drawer. She places several freshly baked loaves of bread and some of the cheese Austin bought that morning into the cloth container. She makes one more decision as she peers at the sky one more time.

"Grab a jacket everyone – it looks like rain. Jonah, please carry the bread and cheese."

"Now we have two St. Nicks," giggle the girls.

Martha grabs a jacket for her husband, who left for the shelter immediately following the noon meal, and sets the pace for the Langly group, walking the three blocks to the shelter. The children don their jackets as it starts to sprinkle. By the time they arrive at the Sharing Table, they notice it is getting colder and that the wind is picking up strength. People on the street, confused by the sudden change in weather, clutch their clothing and hold their crossed arms close to their bodies.

At the shelter, Sarah and Ruth clean the table that gives the shelter its name. When Sunday parishioners come for worship, they often place items on the table for those in need. The table gets a thorough scrubbing each Saturday from the Langly kitchen crew of the week. The rest of the family members do their jobs. Jonah sweeps the premises, while Austin welcomes visitors who come in off the street. Martha, in charge of decorating the front of the sanctuary, rearranges the display. When David hears the family members arrive, he straightens the benches and makes sure all is ready for Sunday worship.

As the family members are working at the shelter, the weather dramatically changes. Within two hours after they left home, the mercury in the thermometer outside drops from 70 to 26 degrees. Austin, who has been outside on the lookout for anyone caught on the street in the rain turning to snow, comes inside.

Periodically, he goes to the door and hollers into the wind, hoping anyone in trouble will be able to follow his voice to shelter.

Martha and David's love for the people of Austin has rubbed off on their oldest son. Austin intentionally selected a place of higher learning in Austin because he wanted to stay close to home. Living at home while attending the university enables the family to remain connected.

While homework is a priority in the Langly household, the children help at the Sharing Table as their schedules allow.

Martha places lanterns on the table and in the window as it darkens inside and out. Several people have found their way to the shelter and all have a story to tell. Austin strikes up a conversation with a thinly clad young man.

"My name is Austin Langly. When I'm not at the shelter or church, I am at the university or studying for classes. What would you like for me to know about you?"

"My name is Thomas Crawford," the visitor replies. "I left my parents and siblings in Tennessee and came to Austin looking for a job. The state capitol building is almost finished. I want to work there as a caretaker to earn enough money for college. Mr. Austin, I am new in this part of the world, can you tell me about this city? Why do you have the same name as the name of the city?"

Austin puts his head back and chuckles.

"Well, Thomas, you would have to ask my parents why they named me Austin," he says, nodding towards his mother. "That is my mother by the sharing table, inviting guests to take some fried bread. However, I have been told that my name was chosen out of appreciation for a place that is home. And yes, I'm named after the founder of this city, Stephen F. Austin. How is that for an expectation to contribute to the community?"

"Your other question has to do with knowing a little something about this city. Stephen Austin's father, Moses, wanted to bring a colony of pioneers from the United States of America to Texas Territory. Moses made a request in 1820 to officials of Spain officially headquartered in San Antonio, Spain's government seat, to bring people to this area. Permission was granted, but he died before he could do so. So his son, Stephen, arranged for 300 families to make the move to Texas Territory. I am a descendant of those original colonists to Austin. They arrived in 1823 and made Austin County the colony's seat of government."

As the men talk, the wind continues to howl and it begins to snow. It gets colder and more wanderers arrive, likely attracted by the lantern in the window. People come inside, stomping the snow off their shoes. David and Martha carry a huge box of clothing left over from the Christmas drive and set it next to the lantern on the sharing table. As she opens the box, Martha notices several sacks of goodies – leftover treats for children on Christmas Eve. She sets the sacks by the bread and cheese, cups her hands around her mouth, and announces, "Gather around to pick out something warm to wear."

The Langly family members help display items from the Christmas box. It seems to be Christmas all over again as they bear witness to hope, joy, and goodwill. People coming in from the street decide to stay until the wind settles down.

The Langlys have noted that the people of Austin have become increasingly intentional about sharing with their needy neighbors. They have been more generous since a hospital physician, in early December, reported to the city council more sickness than usual has been caused by exposure to this cold and damp. Perhaps the Christmas season, combined with an awareness of local need has prompted more activity at the shelter.

Thomas picks out a warm jacket and asks Austin if they can continue their conversation. Austin nods and puts his hand on Thomas' shoulder. "Help me get some benches from the sanctuary for our visitors and then we'll talk some more." They carry the benches to the shelter – and then sit to continue the Austin story.

"So how did the colonists get along with Spain? Did more colonists come to this new land?" asks Thomas.

Austin is happy to continue sharing history.

"In 1824, a year after Austin was established, Mexico gained freedom from Spain and received applications to bring in more colonists. Additional land grants were now issued to Stephen Austin, but by 1830 Mexico stopped immigration to Texas. So many Americans wanted to get into Texas that Mexico became alarmed. Politics in Mexico was unstable. In 1835, a Mexican politician and soldier, Antonio López de Santa Anna, overthrew the Mexican government and made himself dictator."

"I can't imagine the colonists in Texas once lived under a dictator. How did Texas get freed from being ruled by a dictator?" queries Thomas.

"Leaders in Mexico wanted everyone to be a Catholic and they didn't want anyone to own slaves," Austin replies. "Not all people in Texas, however, were abiding by these rules. As a dictator, Santa Anna put force behind any rules he wanted. Many Texans wanted freedom from Mexico, but Mexico didn't honor the request for independence. The Texans were frustrated."

A group gathers around Austin and Thomas.

Austin continues the story. "Six weeks after the defeat following the famous Battle of the Alamo in 1836, Sam Houston and his Texas army surprised Santa Anna and his army at San Jacinto. Santa Anna was captured and forced to relinquish Texas. After Texas declared independence from Mexico in 1836 and became a republic, elections were held. Guess who was elected the first president of Texas? Sam Houston. They wanted to govern their own country of Texas."

"That is totally understandable," Thomas says. "But being their own nation must have had its challenges. When did they become a part of the United States of America – and why?"

Austin explains that, because of its position on slavery, Texas wasn't accepted into the United States of America as a state for almost ten years. "So they ruled themselves as if they were a country, which they were. Texas has had quite a colorful past with six different flags flying over Texas at one time or another: Spain, France, Mexico, Republic of Texas, United States, Confederate States. Texas was accepted to join the United States of America in 1845 and became the twenty-eighth state in the Union. Soon after, the United States and Mexico went to war over other Mexican land holdings the United States wanted to own. I sometimes wonder if Congress accepted Texas as a state simply to be in a position to enlarge the United States landmass."

Martha nods in agreement with her son's thoughts. She then adds her own.

"It seems to me something peaceful could have been worked out rather than killing each other – a purchase of land, the natural settlement of immigrants taking its course, or some type of negotiation. More than 13,000 Americans died in the Mexican-American War."

Martha shakes her head as she cleans up the nearly empty box of Christmas leftover items. The constant drone of the wind draws the people closer together to better hear the sobering story above the din.

"Dissension arose as Americans became embroiled in the approaching Civil War," Austin continues. "Texas joined the slave-holding Confederate states in 1861 to secede from the union. Mother, what do you think would have happened if Abraham Lincoln's Civil War had never been fought?"

"That is hard to say," says Martha. "Maybe the slave-holding states would have seceded and joined together to become their own country. Eventually – hopefully – they would have realized that people can't be owned."

"At least there wouldn't have been all that bloodshed," agrees Austin. "Once the Civil War ended, Reconstruction and rebuilding became a reality. This was not an easy time for Texans. But despite the tensions of the past five years, Texas in 1870 was readmitted to the Union by the United States Congress. And here we are today, the proud state of Texas!"

Everyone applauds and cries of "Yeah!" and a shrill whistle rise above the storm's noisy din.

Thomas looks at his new friend and says, "I think I will like it here in Austin, Austin."

Martha looks into the swirling snow and can't see across the street. "This is a real norther," she says to herself. Southerners use the term "norther" to describe a strong gale of wind from a northerly direction that coincides with a rapidly falling temperature.

"It looks like we'll be here for awhile," Martha says to her daughters. "It's time to slice the bread and cheese."

They set food from the pillowcase on the sharing table. A visitor to the shelter, who decides not to risk going further in the storm, offers cold cuts from her grocery bag. The leftover Christmas sacks of peanuts, pecans, and candy are emptied on the table. And suddenly, the table is filling up. Seemingly out of nowhere, people in the shelter share the food they have, placing it on the sharing table, now transformed into an altar. David asks everyone to gather around the table and reverently offers a simple prayer.

"For these gifts of food, we are truly thankful. Bless all who share with generosity from their storehouse of labor. Bind us together in gratitude as we partake of this food. Amen."

As singing, storytelling, and an impromptu talent show extend into the evening, everyone decides to spend the night at the shelter. The storm is still going strong. The church benches are converted to beds. Everyone at the Sharing Table that night will remember this experience.

The following day, the wind dies, although it is still cold. Everyone has a place to go except Thomas. After helping to clean the shelter, Thomas, now wearing a jacket from the Christmas box, goes home with the Langly family. David stays at the shelter until almost noon in case some brave souls venture out.

Back home, the Langly children do their homework and prepare for Monday lessons. Martha and Thomas visit about his family in Tennessee, his housing needs, and his goal of eventually working at the state capitol.

"I have some ideas," Martha begins.

❋   ❋   ❋

Thomas Crawford endeared himself to the Langlys over the years, becoming like a member of the family. With the help of a matching scholarship, he took night classes at the university, where he majored in horticulture. He went on to work at the state capitol and helped make the capitol building grounds the pride of the city of Austin.

❋   ❋   ❋

The Christian Church of Austin is the oldest congregation of the city, organized in 1847. By 1852, the congregation met for services in a local school building. The congregation belongs to the Disciples of Christ denomination. Its vision statement is "To be a Christ-centered church that supports family, community, and global transformation through worship, education, and outreach." The independent congregation governed itself in a non-hierarchal manner. It selected leaders from among the laity in its first five decades. A congregational split occurred in 1888 over theological and procedural matters. However, a core group continued to honor "In faith, unity; in opinions, liberty; in all things, love." For those remaining, open communion continued to be a part of the worship service..

❋   ❋   ❋

*See Addenda for Chapter 10: "Weather in Texas and Beyond"

❋   ❋   ❋

RECIPE
PECAN SURPRISE COOKIES

(Pecan is the Texas State Tree)
Bake at 300° for 30 minutes.
Yields 2½ dozen

UTENSILS
  Container to melt butter
  Bowl, medium size
  Spoons for measuring
  Spoon for stirring

INGREDIENTS
  Butter 1 cup melted
  Powdered sugar 6 T.
  Flour 2 cups
  Vanilla 1/2 t.
  Almond flavor 1/4 t.
  Pecan halves to place inside each dough ball
  Powdered sugar (extra) for dipping hot baked cookies

METHOD
  Cream butter and powdered sugar.
  Add flour, vanilla, and almond flavoring.
  Blend well.
  Form into small balls.
  Press into each ball of dough ½ pecan.
  Cover the pecan completely.
  Place on cookie sheet; do NOT grease cookie sheet.
  Bake 300° for 30 minutes.
  Dip upper portion of cookies in powdered sugar while hot.

Addenda
Chapter Five: Paul from Saint Paul
(See "Sources and Notes" for Chapter Five)

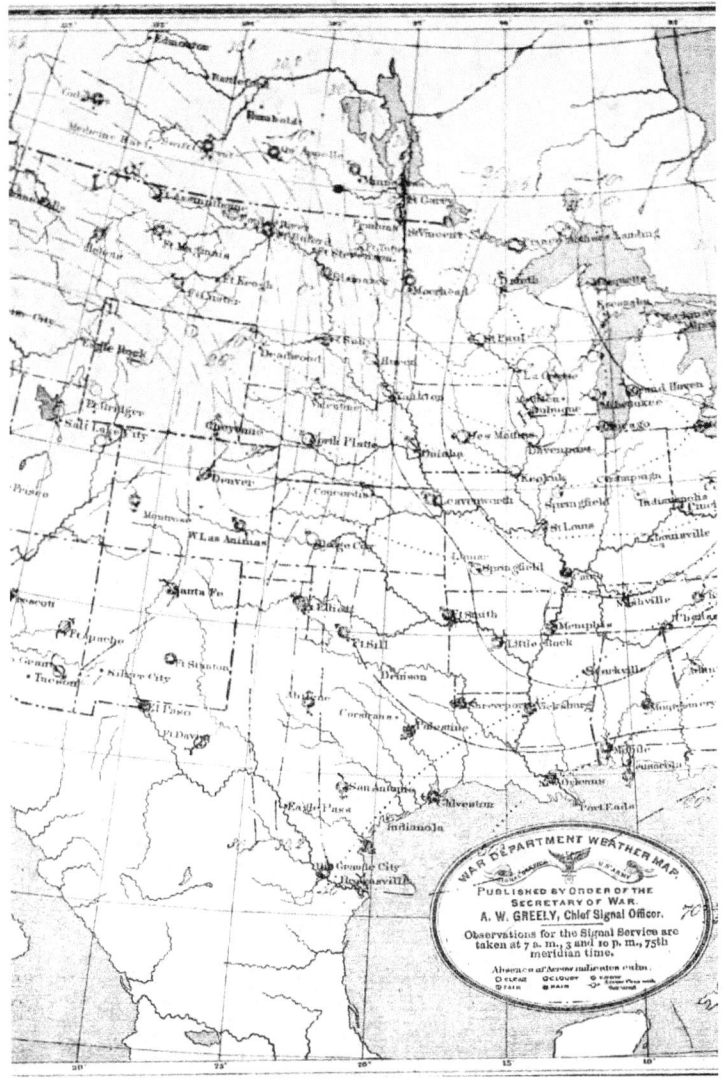

National Weather Map - January 11, 1888
Compliments of NOAA Central Library Data Imaging Project

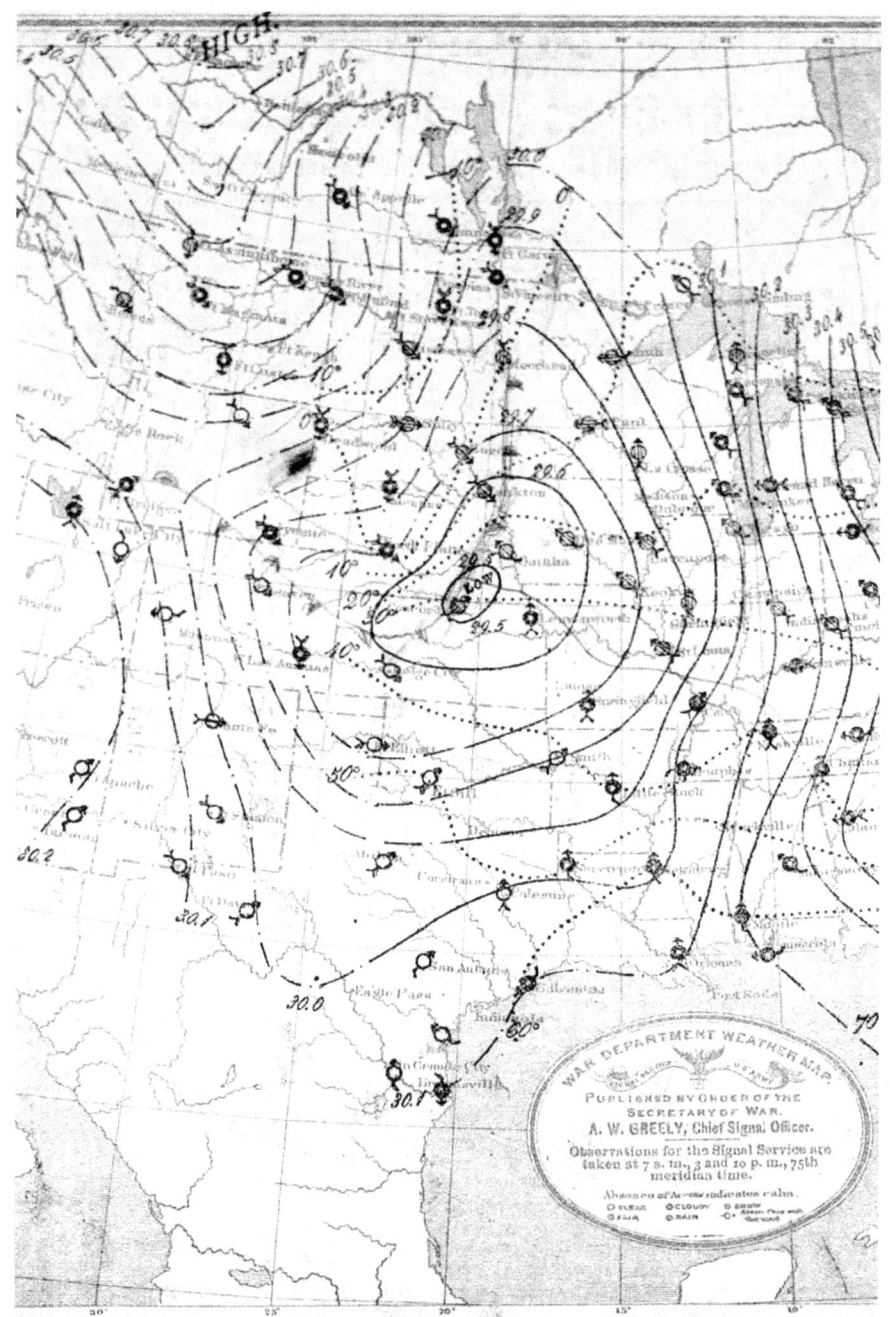

National Weather Map - January 12, 1888
Compliments of NOAA Central Library Data Imaging Project

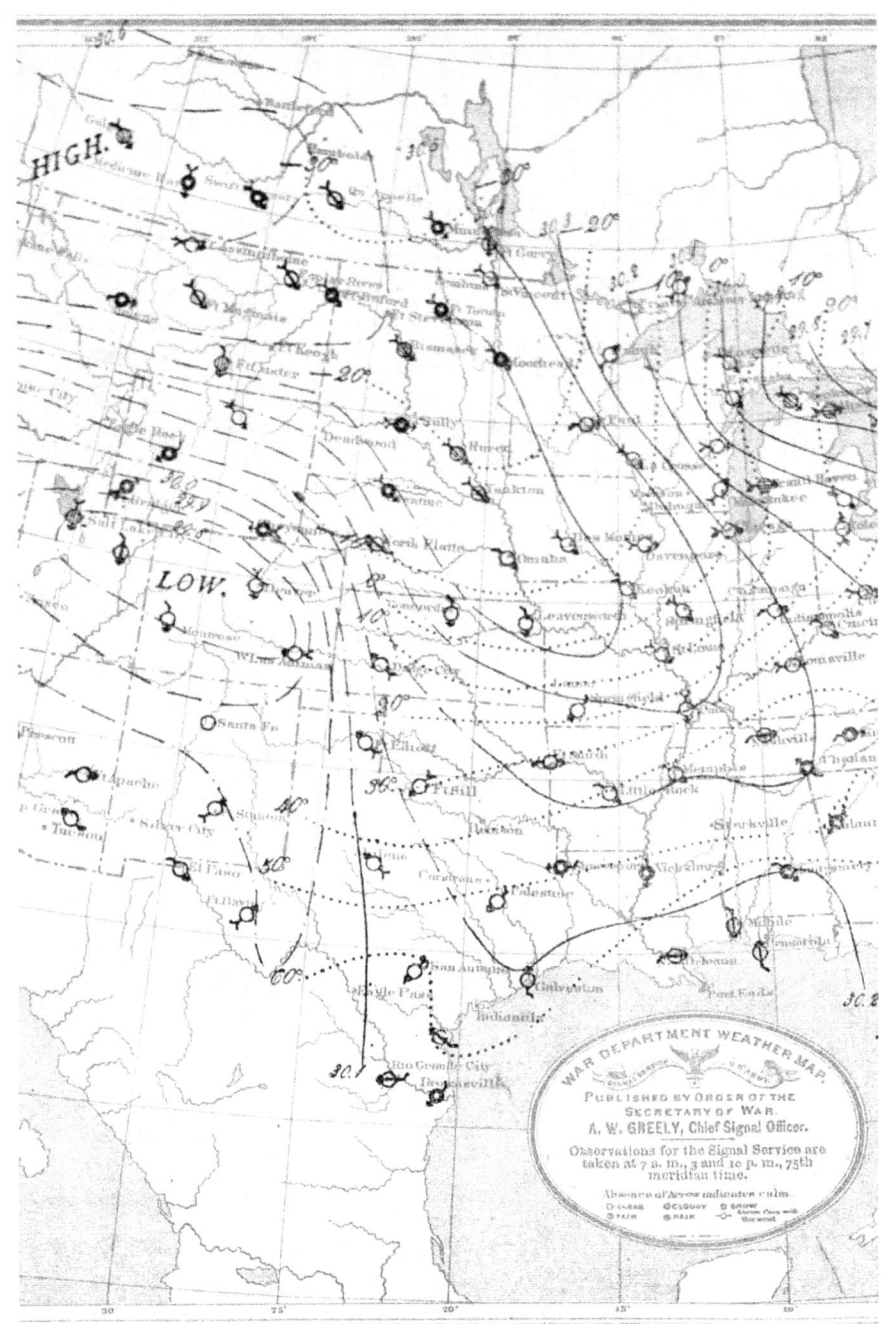

National Weather Map - January 13, 1888
Compliments of NOAA Central Library Data Imaging Project

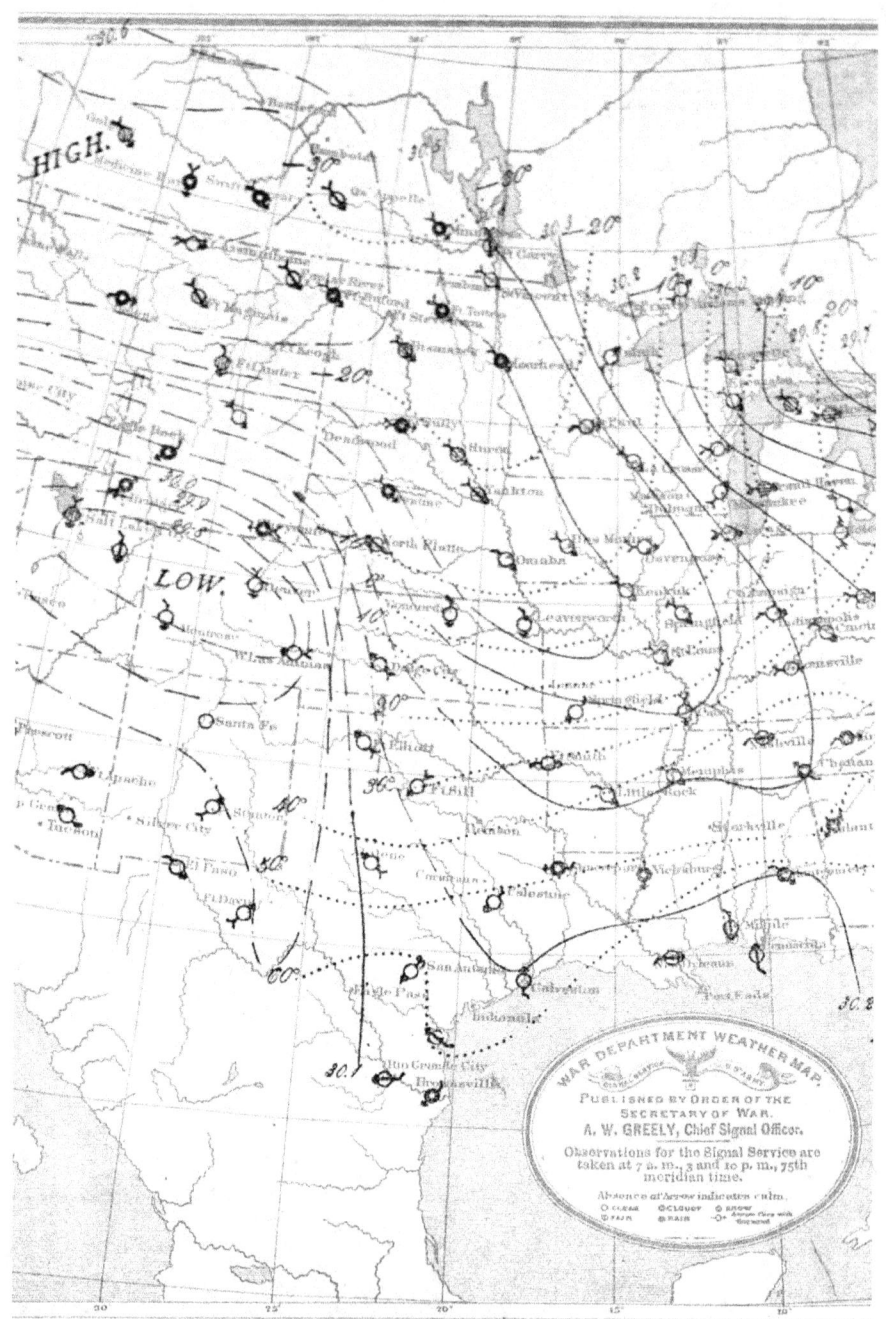

National Weather Map - January 14, 1888
Compliments of NOAA Central Library Data Imaging Project

Chapter Seven: Katharina or Katharine from Henderson and Lena from East of Henderson

(See "Sources and Notes" for Chapter Seven)

Stories of Helen and David Henderson and Their Neighborhood

Helen and David Henderson, for whom the village of Henderson, Nebraska was named, settled on a claim in 1866, three miles south and one-half mile east of the village. They built a large home and hosted many large gatherings, especially for young people. Many immigrants were also welcomed. Their daughter, Janet, was the first woman in York County to register for a marriage license. She married E.D. Copsey on Oct. 26, 1867, the first man in York County to be registered for marriage. They homesteaded in the same section as Janet's parents and brothers, Robert and John. Agnes Henderson married Rowlen Sheperd and Mary married Daniel George. The couples lived in adjoining sections. Nellie, known as Widow Young, and Elizabeth lived at home. Thomas died in infancy.

Before county schools were organized, "subscription schools" were created. Families paid the teacher a per-child monthly fee for schooling. Out of this payment, the teacher paid rent for the school facility. School was conducted in an unused summer log house on the Copsey land. In 1868 and 1869, Mrs. Jarvis Chaffa was the teacher. From 1870 to spring 1876, the residence of Thomas Bearse was used for school purposes. On April 3, 1876, District No. 11 was organized and a school was built across the road to the south from Helen and David's home. David and his neighbors built the school, and by summer, it was in session. The community didn't want the new school empty, so classes started in summer. The Henderson grandchildren lived within walking distance of the school. In the early years, Nellie Henderson taught at District No. 11.

Based on Etta E. Gowey's first-person account
In All Its Fury, p. 317:

Safety During the Storm

January 12, 1888, was a nice warm day, with large flakes of snow coming down rapidly. It was a quiet, still day with no wind at all.

About half-past three in the afternoon, all of a sudden, the wind came up with a terrible roar from the northwest. The snow was blowing so thick and furious that one could not see far at all. Etta E. Gowey was teaching at District No. 11. Mr. Henderson came to the school to get the children and teacher and kept them overnight at his home. Most of the children were the Hendersons' grandchildren. Etta's sister, Minnie Gowey, taught at Lushton, a few miles to the east. She stayed at the schoolhouse all night. The big boys kept the fire going in the school-house with coal and cobs. She had forty pupils.

Based on E.J. Walters' first-person account
In All Its Fury, pp. 307-308:

Corncobs, Rope, and Supper

Seeley School, District No. 20, another country school, was located two and one-half miles southeast of District No. 11 across the road from Orlando H. Darling's property; it was known as the "Darling School." The wood frame schoolhouse sat a half-mile north of what is known as the "Seeley Mill" on the Blue River. The teacher, Libbie Ramsey, asked E.J. Walters, a nineteen-year-old student and the oldest of the twenty in attendance that day, to bring fuel into the school-house. She raised the window and asked E.J. and another student to crawl through and throw corncobs back in. Two loads of cobs had been delivered and unloaded under the window on the south side of the schoolhouse the previous day.

One father came for his son and took him home. They had to go north and face the storm for half-a-mile. The boy almost suffocated – his face was covered by a scarf, but the snow sifted through the fabric and was tightly packed against his nose and mouth. They made it home safely by staying between two fences used as an alley-way to move livestock to a different field.

In the evening, William Wilkes, who lived on the Darling place, crossed the road to the schoolhouse, bringing a rope. He told all the pupils and the teacher to take a hold of the rope and to be sure not to let loose. He led the way with the teacher in the center and E.J. at the end. It was difficult, but everyone held on and they all reached the house. Mrs. Wilkes was waiting for everyone to arrive; she had pre-pared a meal. After supper, Mr. Wilkes took the teacher and the older pupils back to the schoolhouse but kept the smaller ones at his home until the next day. Everyone in that district was safe.

History and Development of the Word "Blizzard" in the Nineteenth Century

1830: Davy Crockett
When having fun at another's expense such as when giving a toast: "He gave him a blizzard."

1834: Davy Crockett
The Life and Adventures of Colonel David Crockett of West Tennessee Almanacs (1834) When firing a cannon, a rifle shot, or multiple shots: "I saw two more bucks . . . I took a blizzard at one of them and up he tumbled."

1860: Verbal blast or an exclamation: "giving him the blazes"

1870: Iowa newspaper describes a blizzard: "a violent storm with powdery, driving snow, and extremely cold winds"

1870: England: corruption of "blazing hard"

1890: Stunning blow
An 1890 entry in *Slang and Its Analogues* by J.S. Farmer & W.E. Henley: Merciless in ridicule during debate; "gave his opponent a blizzard"

Chapter Eight: Gertrune from Newton

(See "Sources and Notes" for Chapter Eight)

More Survival Stories of Kansas Students and Teachers During the January 12, 1888 Blizzard

Stories of decisions by teachers to keep their pupils safe during the January 12, 1888 blizzard varied, given the timing, circumstances, and resources. Stories in *In All Its Fury: The Great Blizzard of 1888* preserve firsthand accounts of myriads of methods for survival.

Based on Geo. M. Lovell's first-person account
In All Its Fury, p. 97:

Trusting Older Boys

Geo. M. Lovell, a teacher in a country school near Axtell, Kansas, near the Nebraska border, had twenty students at school that day, January 12, 1888. School was dismissed at the onset of the storm. Mr. Lovell was confident all could reach their homes safely, except for the two small German boys who had one-and-a-half miles to go. Two larger Swedish boys volunteered to walk them safely home.

When all the pupils had gone, and the teacher was preparing to leave, the father of the two German boys stepped inside the schoolhouse, asking for his children. Mr. Lovell explained that the Johnson brothers had offered to see his sons home. The father quickly concluded they must have taken the shortcut through the woods, but no one was sure.

It was an awful night for Mr. Lovell. He reached his boardinghouse alright, but he could not eat and worry kept him from sleeping. After the storm died, Mr. Lovell learned all the pupils had reached home safely.

Based on Zella Masten's first-person account
In All Its Fury, pp. 98-99:

A Rope Behind the Back

Zella Masten, attending District No. 73 in Washington County, Kansas, was nine years old at the time of the blizzard. The teacher rang the afternoon recess bell. Just as Zella stopped to pick up a snowball, the storm struck so suddenly that the teacher couldn't see Zella. The teacher called and called her name. Finally, they found each other.

A school board member urged everyone to go home because there was hardly any fuel left. A neighbor, Mr. May, arrived to get his two sons and Zella and her two brothers. One end of a long rope was tied to Mr. May's belt and the other to his older son's belt. The remaining four pupils walked with the rope at their backs. They followed a fence. Ever so often, the group would stop and turn to the south to catch their breath. What a relief to make it home.

Based on Pearl F. Rickey's first-person account
In All Its Fury, pp. 104-105:

Curtains and a Barbed Wire Fence

Miss Agnes Algie taught in the Hatch District. It was later known as the Farmington District, located four miles northwest of Washington, Kansas. She and her pupils were caught at the school during the blizzard with insufficient food, clothing, and fuel.

The older boys brought in the last four chunks of wood. No corncobs were left. The big boys used the stove poker to break up the benches, but they were made of light wood and burned quickly. They all gathered around the potbelly stove, watching the last of the embers die out. Miss Algie decided the best alternative was to go to the Hatch residence half-a-mile away. As the embers faded, it grew darker and colder. They had to hurry.

Miss Algie tore curtains to make scarves to tie over the youngest students' faces. They formed a human chain so as to not get separated. With her free hand, Miss Algie held onto and followed the barbed wire fence. She led the pupils through the dark and into the blinding, swirling snow. The cold blizzard penetrated through their clothing, leaving everyone chilled.

After what seemed like a very long time, they finally reached the Hatch home, where they were snugly sheltered. The next problem? How to notify the frantic parents, anxious about their children's whereabouts. In due time, all were contacted and told their children were safe.

Bernhard Warkentin Jr. and the Economics of Turkey Red Winter Wheat

Bernhard Warkentin Jr. was born June 18, 1847, at Altonau, Molotschna Colony, South Russia. He attended school in Ohrloff and Halbstadt, Molotschna Colony, and attended business college in Odessa. As a thirteen-year-old, he was aware of the village farming practices. He watched his father, Bernhard Aron Warkentin Sr., and his farming methods with interest. The elder Warkentin introduced the Turkey red hard winter wheat into the South Russian soil, resulting in improved productivity. The younger Warkentin's desire was to find other places to introduce this fine seed.

When Bernhard was twenty-five, he and three friends traveled six months and more than 1,500 miles throughout the mid-United States and Canada in search of suitable land to sow the valued wheat seed. Warkentin communicated with people back in the Old Country and wrote to his friend, David Goerz. He told him the soil and climate in Kansas were similar to that of South Russia. He recommended Kansas as a place for emigrants from his homeland. He also instructed they should bring along the wheat seed.

In 1874, Warkentin bought two sections of land in Harvey County. He built a gristmill at Halstead and processed ten barrels of flour a day. Wheat production kept improving. In 1870, Kansans raised 2.5 million bushels of spring wheat. By 1880, following the introduction of Turkey red hard winter wheat, 17.3 million bushels were raised. By 1890, the number climbed to 30.3 million.

As a landowner and a businessman at Halstead, Bernhard supervised the gristmill for eleven years; flour was processed daily. In 1885, Warkentin sold the Halstead Milling & Elevator Company.

With the sale of his investment, Bernhard and his wife proceeded to travel with their family to Europe and South Russia to visit relatives. He arranged to import 10,000 bushels of Turkey red hard winter wheat seed from South Russia to Kansas. The following year, he purchased Monarch Steam Mill in Newton. This Romanesque building along Main Street near the railroad tracks was built in 1879. The roof has a mansard-style architecture topping the fourth floor. The building was renamed the Newton Milling and Elevator Company. The same year that Warkentin purchased the Newton Mill, he began building the Victorian home for himself and his wife, Wilhelmina, on First Street in Newton. While in Europe, they hand-selected Italian tile, Czechoslovakian crystal chandeliers, and more for their new home. It was completed in 1887. The Warkentin family certainly added "class" to the community.

Schools

One month after deciding to build the Kellas schoolhouse, the school board met. At its October 10, 1873, meeting, the board approved the expenditures for the school building totaling $534; expenses were under budget. Hatfield and Hereick, patrons of the district, were paid $415 for building the twenty-two-by-sixteen-foot school, with $10 earmarked for Ensign & Brooks to supply the limestone rock used in the foundation. And $2.50 went to Mr. Marks for masonry work, $88.50 to J.C. Brooks for school furniture, and $18 to Mr. Lehman for the stove and pipe. Mr. Kellas served as treasurer (for the next thirty-two years) of the newly organized school.

Kellas District No. 35 wasn't the first school in the Newton area. Newton's first school began September 2, 1872, the year before the Kellas school was built. The school term was three months, with Mary A. Boyd as the teacher. The school was conducted in an area above the Burnhisel Harness Shop in the Ringolsky Building on the east side of Main Street between Fifth and Sixth Streets. That same year, the community passed a $5,000 bond issue to build a wood frame school on Oak Street between Seventh and Eighth Streets that was known as Garfield School.

Chapter Nine: Edith from Enid

(See "Sources and Notes" for Chapter Nine)

Education in Indian Territory

Children of ranchers in the Cherokee Outlet had limited options for an education. There was no free public school in Indian Territory until Oklahoma Territory was established in 1890. Education was random when done at home. Another option was for children to attend a "subscription school," where payment per pupil was made to the teacher. That method of education depended on the parents' ability to pay the monthly tuition.

The Native American tribes had an excellent educational system before coming to Indian Territory. The Cherokee people followed the methods of teaching from Sequoya, one of their own people. In 1821 Sequoya invented a system of writing. This method brought results in just a few weeks. But education for the indigenous people now living on reservations in Indian Territory underwent a change.

The United States government paid religious orders to provide schooling for Native American children living on reservations. In 1879, one entrepreneur, Joseph W. Scroggs, a Congregational minister, organized a school in the Cherokee Nation of Indian Territory. It was also open to white children. But these residential schools deprived the Native Americans of much of their dignity.

Students were expected to conform to the "European" culture while attending residential schools. Hair was cut. Names were changed to English. Speaking their native language was prohibited. Any aspect of Indian culture was not tolerated. This seriously damaged the self-esteem of many indigenous people. Living away from family resulted in loneliness and isolation. Parents were not allowed to visit. There were no home visits. Discipline was harsh. Children were overworked in tasks expected of them. This physical and emotional abuse took its toll. Illness often went untreated and children died. Parents were often not informed until months later. There was sexual abuse. In one case, after a nine-year-old girl was molested by her teacher, the girls bunched together with several to a bed. The girls clung to each other in fear and for a sense of safety.

One can only – or perhaps cannot begin to – imagine how these children kept warm during the blizzard of January 12, 1888.

The last residential school closed in 1973.

Chapter 10: Austin from Austin

(See "Sources and Notes" for Chapter Ten)

Weather in Texas and Beyond:
January 14, 15, 16, 1888

Abilene, Texas

January 14, 1888:10 a.m. A norther with temperature falling to -2.

January 15, 1888: 7 a.m. It is -5.

Austin, Texas

January 15, 1888: The high is 18 degrees and the low is -6.

January 16, 1888: The Colorado River freezes over for the first time since the colonists arrive in 1823.

Brownsville, Texas

January 15, 1888: 7 a.m. Increasing wind to 34 miles per hour at 11 p.m. Low for the day is 23 degrees.

January 16, 1888: 9 a.m. Severe norther. Low for the day is 21. Trees and fences are covered with one inch of ice.

Corpus Christi, Texas

January 15, 1888: 2 a.m. Temperatures fall from 60 at 2 a.m. to 16 during the day. Wind is up to 36 miles per hour.

Fort Elliott. Texas

January 14, 1888: 3 a.m. The average temperature is -7. Wind is 48 miles per hour.

January 15, 1888: 7 a.m. It is -14 degrees. Wind is 40 miles per hour from the north.

Galveston, Texas

January 15, 1888: 1 a.m. The wind shifts to the northwest with a velocity of a storm. Rain changes to snow at 4 a.m. Temperature is below freezing. The fine snow and frozen mist become needles of ice. Telephone and telegraph wires encased in ice, crash, cutting the city from the mainland for twenty-four hours.

Rio Grande City, Texas

January 15, 1888: 5:45 a.m. Falling rain freezes.

California

January 14-18, 1888: Frost and ice form, a most unusual occurrence.

Los Angeles, California

January 15, 1888: High is 32 degrees with heavy frost and ice.

San Francisco, California

January 15, 1888: Water pipes freeze. Ice is four inches thick.

January 16, 1888: Light snow.

Summit, Mississippi

January 16, 1888: The ground is covered with sleet, snow, and ice. The coldest weather of the season penetrates the entire state.

Sources and Notes

Chapter One: Eddie from Edmonton

Juhnke, J., and Hunter, C. *The Missing Peace: The Search for Nonviolent Alternatives in United States History*. Kitchener, Ontario: Pandora Press, 2001, pp. 78, 162, 173.

> Addressing a perspective that is normal for one party and not the other takes courage to acknowledge and sort through. James Juhnke and Carol Hunter describe the work required in a relationship of valued partnership that is important to the well-being of both parties.

Kerr, D., and Hanson, S. *Saskatoon, the First Half-Century*. Edmonton, Alberta: NeWest Press, 1982, p. 25.

> Don Kerr and Stan Hanson use the term "hit and miss" to describe when school is in session. It depended very much on the teacher in those earlier years. This quip applied to what happened regarding schools in session in Canada – beyond Alberta – as well as on the Great Plains of the United States.

McDougall, W.D. "Edmonton." *World Book Encyclopedia*, Vol. 6, 1971. Chicago: Field Enterprises Educational Corporation, p. 55.

> This article helped me get acquainted with the city and the early days of existence.

King, S., and Richards, J. Howard. "Schools." *World Book Encyclopedia*, Vol. 17, 1971, p. 122.

> Churches and missions provided schooling before the federal government in 1884 stepped in with recommendations. Stirling King and J. Howard Richards clarified for me the schooling expectations that attempted to regulate the educational system. School was for children ages seven to twelve, and attendance was for twelve weeks.

Murchie, G. "How Air Works for Us." *World Book Encyclopedia*, Vol. 1, 1971, pp. 154-158.

> Guy Murchie is quite detailed in the dynamics of air movement. The use of a straw is explained.

> Air pressure is caused by the weight of air from the top of the atmosphere as it presses down upon the layers of air below. When sucking whey or any liquid through a straw, air pressure works for

you. You then remove the air from inside the straw. This lets the pressure of the air outside the straw push the liquid upward into your mouth. An instrument for measuring air pressure is called a barometer and the pressure of air is measured in inches of mercury.

By definition, a barometer measures the effect of the sun causing air to move by being heated. When air is heated, it expands and becomes lighter. It then rises like a huge, invisible balloon. The warm air is pushed by the cooler, heavier air that moves in to take its place. This kind of motion is the cause of wind.

The Earth's Water Cycle. Map/chart. NASA, 2007.

A visual is an added learning device.

Snaddon, A. "Alberta." *World Book Encyclopedia*, Vol. 1, 1971, pp. 297, 314.

Alberta was a part of the North-West Territories before being designated as a district in anticipation of becoming a province one day. The process of organization, governance, and development of a vast area was complex. Settlers were eager to use the land and streams.

Waite, P.B. "Rebellion." *World Book Encyclopedia*, Vol. 17, 1971, p. 127.

The rebellion had much to do with fairness in treating the *Metis* people of French and Native American parentage. Land ownership and representation in government were the desired outcome of the rebellion.

Chapter Two: June from Saskatoon

Cronkite, F.C. "Saskatoon." *World Book Encyclopedia*, Vol. 17, 1971, pp. 127, 124c, 124f.

Saskatoon was founded in 1882 by John N. Lake (p. 127).

The information regarding weather is gleaned from p. 124c.

Railroads were built across Saskatchewan in 1882-83 (p. 124f).

Ewers, J.C. "Assiniboin Indians." *World Book Encyclopedia*, Vol. 1, 1971, p. 776.

I drew on John C. Ewers' research on life with the Assiniboin people as they moved around between the Missouri and Saskatchewan Rivers hunting and trading.

Saskatchewan Herald (Battleford, Sask.), January 14, 1888, p. 1, "A Bit of a Blizzard."

The below-freezing temperatures and Mr. Mears' encounter with the storm indicate conditions were quite unfavorable.

Snaddon, A. "Alberta." *World Book Encyclopedia*, Vol. 1, 1971, p. 297.

Andrew Snaddon and his colleagues, L.G. Thomas and William C. Wonders, were helpful in understanding the division of the region in 1882 between Manitoba and British Columbia. It was divided into four territorial districts: Alberta, Assiniboia, Athabaska and Saskatchewan.

Chapter Three: Helen from Helena

Chaffee, O. (1971). "Schools." *World Book Encyclopedia*, Vol.13, 1971, p. 628.

Oscar Chaffee notes that before Montana became a state, school organization was left to communities and private tutors.

Laskin, D. *The Children's Blizzard*. New York: HarperCollins, 2004, pp. 87, 125.

A definition of a cold wave and the description of a cold wave flag renders authenticity.

Michener, J. *Centennial*. Connecticut: Fawcett Publications, Inc., 1974, pp. 725-27.

Recalling James Michener's penchant for detail, I reread *Centennial* to vicariously experience the winters of Montana. The description regarding how different animals respond differently to snow is interesting. From experience, I know cattle drift with the wind, especially when the momentum of herd mentality crashes through the best of maintained fences. The fences in 1888 were relatively new, having been put up by October 1886, when the open-range laws went into effect.

O'Gara, W. *In All Its Fury: The Great Blizzard of 1888*. Lincoln, Neb.: Union College Press, 1947, p. 105.

Mrs. Della J. Robinson, living at Edmond, Kansas during the blizzard of 1888, recounts how the cattle driven by the storm were too weak to go further and were found dead in piles after the snow melted. It was her daughter who was teaching in Birney, Montana in 1919 who was reminded of the 1888 blizzard and to dismiss school if it would begin to snow hard.

Chapter Four: Mark from Bismarck

Almond, G. (1971). "Bismarck." *World Book Encyclopedia*, Vol. 2, 1971, p. 301.

> This resource includes the beginning of Bismarck and its namesake.

Hagerty, J. (1971). "North Dakota." *World Book Encyclopedia*, Vol. 14, 1971, pp. 386, 393-97.

> The northern part of Dakota Territory had a distinctive culture in comparison to the southern part of the territory. I found it helpful to understand the background of the settlers as they pioneered in Dakota Territory, bringing their culture with them.

Laskin, *The Children's Blizzard*, pp. 115, 122.

> A duplication of weather in Helena would reach Bismarck in eight hours 71 percent of the time.

> Laskin's story of Mr. Brown, the station agent, is compelling. The weather forecast inspired Brown in a noble effort to save lives of children.

Chapter Five: Paul from Saint Paul

Laskin, *The Children's Blizzard*, pp. 85-89, 97-98, 101, 107-116.

> I am indebted to David Laskin for writing *The Children's Blizzard*. The comprehensive description surrounding weather is carefully researched. His time spent interviewing relatives was helpful to my understanding of the personalities in this story.

> With this information, I imagined what life was like for the characters in this chapter. Thank you, David Laskin.

NOAA Climate Database Modernization Program. National Climatic Data Center, Asheville, NC.

> For further assistance in translating the maps, please contact: Library.Reference@noaa.gov, 301-713-2600 ext. 157.

St. Paul (Minn.) Daily Globe, January 14, 1888, p. 1, "Casualties Reported in Dakota, Nebraska, Iowa, and Minnesota."

Taylor, G. "The Barometer and the Weather." *World Book Encyclopedia*, Vol. 2, 1971, pp. 83-84.

> Research connecting air pressure and arthritis is ongoing. The description of decreased pressure of air in body cells pushing outward against sensitive skin is one explanation.

Chapter Six: Maria or Mariean from Freeman

Centennial Homestead Map and Supplement (1874-1974).

The information on the map records that Mr. Goertz's boys found the five frozen bodies on Sunday morning, January 15, 1888.

Graber, A. *Swiss Mennonite Ancestors and Their Relationship from 1775.* Freeman, S.D.: Pine Hill Press, 1980, pp. 10, 83, 133, 184, 244, 456.

Arthur Graber's genealogy records include the three families in this chapter on pages 10, 184, and 244. On page 456 is the genealogy of Rev. Johann Schrag (the great-great-great-grandpa of my husband, Ron), former pastor of Salem Church. Anna (mother of the three frozen Kaufman boys) is Schrag's daughter. Her older brother, Joseph, is Ron's great-great-grandpa.

The Goertz family, from the Low German ethnic group, is in this genealogy book on page 83. Perhaps the reason for inclusion is because three sons married women of Swiss ancestry.

In studying the genealogy, I notice Maria Graber Albrecht's father, Jacob, is a brother to Peter O. Graber. This means Maria and frozen Peter are first cousins. Maria's son, frozen John (born on the ship), and frozen Peter are first cousins once removed (p. 133).

Graber, E. *Memoirs of Rev. John Schrag and Family.* Privately printed, 1952, pp. 16-17, 45-47.

The editor, Edwin P. Graber, preserves A.P. Graber's first-person account of the blizzard on pages 45-47. Andreas (A.P.) is the oldest son of Peter O. Graber and Susanna, Peter's new wife. His reference to Widow Goertzen, (Goertz) with her three big boys who didn't know to whom the frozen boys belonged, was curious information. Who was the third big boy? Widow Goertz was Katherine (Frank) Tieszen. The Heritage Hall Archives in Freeman, South Dakota provided genealogy information about Frank and Katherine Weisz Tieszen. They had eight children, four of whom grew to adulthood. Katherine Tieszen married Johann Goertz May 11, 1875. (Goertz's first wife, Katherina Neufeld Goertz died en route to America and was buried at sea July 1874, A. Graber, 1980, p. 83.) Katherine Tieszen brought to the marriage four children: Peter F., born in 1863, Anna F., born in 1870, Katherine F., born in 1871, and Frank F., born in 1872. Sometime during 1888, Frank turned sixteen. It is possible that Frank F. Tieszen was with his stepbrothers Henry Goertz, fifteen, and Peter Goertz, seventeen, when the frozen boys were discovered.

Graber, J. "Remembrances of Pioneer Life." Unpublished presentation for the 75th anniversary of the Salem-Zion Mennonite Church, September 4, 1955.

> Jacob D. Graber, the author, was eleven years old when he left his school in Childstown Township to go three-fourths of a mile home. His father set out to meet him, shouting his name. Low visibility could have caused father and son to miss each other, but his father kept shouting his name, and they found each other. Jacob's school was five-and-one-half miles southwest from District No. 66. The weather conditions of zero visibility were similar.

Kauffman, J. (2018). *Kauffman: Three Merchants of Integrity*. Hillsboro, Kan.: Free Press Books, 2018, pp. 96-106.

> James Kauffman shares family stories, and includes the following incident that adds grief to Johann Kaufman's life: The following year (1889) in summer, Johann Kaufman had a grass mowing accident. Benjamin Kaufman, only three-and-a-half years old, couldn't get out of his uncle's way fast enough, and his left foot was cut off by the mower. Johann Kaufman died in 1890 at age forty-five.

Kaufmann, P.R.; trans. Reuben Peterson, May 1979, Basil, Kan. *Our People and Their History*. Sioux Falls, S.D.: Augustana College, 1931.

> The origin of family names, and the Volhynian villages from which they came, are listed.

Schrag, M. *The European History of the Swiss Mennonites from Volhynia*. North Newton, Kan.: Mennonite Press, 1974, pp. 78, 82.

> Martin Schrag reviews the reasons for leaving Russia: Russian language in schools and spoken everywhere; militarization for all men; worship mandated in the Russian Orthodox tradition (p. 78).

> Names of the seven villages emigrating from Volhynia are listed (p. 82).

Stoddard, W. *Turner County Pioneer History*. South Dakota: Brown & Saenger, 1931, pp. 200, 207-209.

> W. H. Stoddard reviews many memorable storms for the *Sioux City Journal*, January 10, 1926, page 200. Storm survivor Peter J. Albrecht's remembrance of the storm in "A Fatal Day" is printed on pages 207-209. This is where the quote,"I hope you boys will not be absent" from Mr. Cotton, the teacher, originates. Also in this piece, Mr. Goertz's boys find the five children, but they don't know to whom they belong. And Peter writes that one father says,

with agony in his soul, "Oh God, is it mine or Thine fault that I find my three boys frozen like the beasts of the field?"

Stucky, H. Mennonite Ship List: Swiss (Volhynian) 1874 of the Immigrants Who Came From Russia. North Newton, Kan.: Mennonite Press Inc., 1974, pp. 11-29.

Harley Stucky provides a record of family names on specified ships.

The Swiss-Germans in South Dakota: From Volhynia to Dakota Territory. Freeman, S.D.: Pine Hill Press, 1974, pp. 21, 36, 40-41.

Life of the Swiss-Germans is described as they transition to farming in America (page 21). A review of the reasons for emigrating to America give the same as those mentioned in other sources (page 36). It seems allegiance to the czar rather than God was required for those staying in Russia. Thus, it was paramount that the group move within the ten-year time frame. Pages 40-41 tell about early funerals in Dakota.

Waltner, E. *Banished for Faith*. Freeman, S.D.: Pine Hill Press, 1968, p. 185.

Emil Waltner reviews the new policy in Russia, an edict that prompted the emigration to America.

Waltner, P.J.; trans. Sieglinda Waltner Preheim. *I Consider the Days of Old*. Private printing, June 30, 2000, pp. 12, 17, 27.

The conversation between Peter Jos Waltner and his mother regarding *kuchen* (page 12) shows the delight of a child's favorite food in Volhynia. Kuchen continues to be a favorite of all ages among the Swiss-German people. (Sieglinda Waltner Preheim, P.J. Waltner's granddaughter, translated the German script.)

Zehr, O. Pseudobulbar Effect. Rochester, Minn.: Mayo Clinic, May 14, 2020.

Justina Neufeld, friend of the author, checked with her colleague, Orlyn Zehr, also in the field of psychiatry, to name the episode of Anna's sudden uncontrollable and inappropriate laughter. "The Pseudobulbar Effect typically occurs in people with a certain neurological condition or injury. The milder response may be just a matter of displacement." Anna likely experienced a milder response. The displacement was a matter of not being able to deal directly with the tragedy of seeing her three frozen sons. The emotions overcompensated with an inappropriate response.

Chapter Seven: Katherina or Katharine from Henderson and Lena from East of Henderson

Friesen, E. Telephone interview by the author, April 8, 2016.

I learned from Elmer about customs regarding where haystacks are placed and about mule instincts.

Friesen, J.J. *Incidents of Pioneer Life.* Unpublished.

This is valuable firsthand insight and experience to early pioneer living, education, and family life as it pertains to the Jacob and Anna Friesen family. This handwritten paper explains the attendance of school (three days of "English" school with Fanny White as teacher) with ongoing German school taught in homes.

Friesen, M. The Jacob and Anna Friesen Family. Unpublished presentation, July 1999.

Marion Friesen provided me with maps and genealogy charts. LeRoy and Marion Friesen provided a guided tour of homesteads.

Henderson-landmark-disappearing. http://heartlandbeat.com.

Evidence of the timber hedge remains today. Reading about the son's and grandson's memories of this *volt* (woods), prompted me to learn more about the Timber Culture Act of 1873. Likely, there were fourteen rows, twelve feet apart – the length of a half-mile.

Henderson (Neb.) News, December 31, 1987, p. 3, "Centennial Clippings."

Inez Pankratz Epp penned the story of the 1888 blizzard in Henderson for correspondent Martha Friesen. Friesen quotes Fiegenbaum regarding his blizzard experience in Hampton.

History and Development of the Word "Blizzard" in the Nineteenth Century. (https://english.blogoverflow.com)

History of York County, Nebraska, Vol. 1. "The Blizzard of 1888." Chicago: J.J. Clarke Publishing Co., 1921, pp. 341-42.

Janzen, E. Telephone interview by the author, April 8, 2016.

Elva Janzen provided verification of the value of the shortcut that meant the horses wouldn't have to negotiate the steep railroad bed for crossing. Elva lived close to the railroad track, and as a child she followed the tracks to school. Her grandparents lived nearby.

Laskin, *The Children's Blizzard,* pp. 32-34, 148-151, 248-251, 263-264.

David Laskin's research fills in details of Lena Woebbecke's life.

O'Gara, *In All Its Fury*, pp. 53, 117-118, 307-08, 317.

The forward thinking of William O'Gara, collecting stories of those in the January 12, 1888 blizzard, is a valuable resource.

Plat map for York County. (1889).

Sod houses, homes, tree claims, railroad tracks, land ownership, and organized school districts are a part of the legend.

Sedwick, T.E. *York County Nebraska and Its People, Vol. II*. Chicago: J.J. Clarke Publishing Co., 1921, p. 896.

An account of David Henderson's family helps match Henderson's daughters to their married names and subsequently to land ownership on the plat map. This explains why pupils of District No. 11 are mostly grandchildren of David and Helen Henderson.

Siebert, C., guided tour, 2017.

Carl Siebert conducted a guided tour of his neighborhood, including Seeley Mill, Darling School, Lushton, David and Helen Henderson's homestead, and the location of District No. 11 across the road.

Thieszen, H. Telephone interview by the author, March 14, 2020.

Harold Thieszen checked his *Weadbuck* (word book) collection for the *Plautdietsche* (Low German) spelling of roasted zwieback: *reesche tweeback*.

"Timber Culture Act." Wikipedia, 12-28-2019.

According to Wikipedia, of the nearly 9 million acres entered as tree claims in Nebraska, about 2.5 million acres were approved for a 160-acre deed. This act was repealed in 1891.

Schedule for planting ten acres of trees:

Year One – Plow five acres

Year Two – Cultivate; plow another five acres

Year Three – Plant the Year One plowed field; cultivate the Year Two plowed field

Year Four – Plant the Year Two cultivation

Voth, S. *Henderson Mennonites: From Holland to Henderson*. "Education and Community Schools," pp. 87-99; "From Russia to America – The Great Migration," pp.19-40. Henderson, Neb.: Service Press, 2000.

Stanley Voth, editor, pulls together many aspects of history of the Henderson community. As background in the life of the pioneers

emigrating from Russia who settled around Henderson, this resource tells a story of vision and hope for a quiet way of life among
family and friends.

York (Neb.) Republican, January 25, 1888, p. 2, "Correspondence:
Henderson's Clippings."

The railroad went through Henderson in 1888, and the article
documents the accident in addition to the snow giving cause for a
delay in January.

Young, N. "David Henderson," in *Old Settlers Early History of York
County, Nebraska.* York, Neb.: Officers of Old Settlers Early History,
1913, pp. 156-59.

Reading Nellie Young's account of her Henderson family is indeed helpful in putting pieces of the puzzle together regarding life
during pioneer days. It is this article that prompts me to wonder
about schooling for David Henderson's family before District No.
11 was organized.

Chapter Eight: Gertrune from Newton

**Nineteenth Amendment Centennial: The Official Kansas Suffrage
Celebration.** Brochure. August 13-15, 2020.

Kansas in many ways was a leader in paving the way for equality.
Being the eighth state to extend equal voting rights to women in
1912 and the fourth state to ratify the Nineteenth Amendment,
June 16, 1919, Kansas modeled a place for gender equality. On
August 18, 1920, Congress ratified the Nineteenth Amendment
to the United States Constitution.

Fundamentals of Poetry. Chicago: Language Kit Company, 1963, pp.
1, 3, 7-8.

This four-by-six-inch booklet of thirty-one pages is a treasured
jewel, although I have no recollection of how I came to possess
such a gem. It helped me recognize different types of poetry.

Globe, January 17, 1888, p. 1, "The Blizzard Victims." ProQuest Historical Newspapers: The Globe and Mail.

The Kansas spirit of reaching out and helping others is a tribute to
the humanity of early pioneers.

Harvey County Museum and Archives, Newton, Kansas

Sifting through contents of boxes, I viewed records and maps.
Books were available to read. Staff at the Harvey County Museum

and Archives allowed me time to sit in the Kellas School building at a double desk and reconnect with my former country school experiences. This helped me remember those days.

"K is for Kansas: Exploring Kansas from A to Z." Kauffman Museum traveling exhibition, 2015.

Kauffman Museum, North Newton, Kan., transports me through time and place. A pamphlet printed by Mennonite Press of Newton in 2015 captures the essence of "K is for Kansas."

Kellas School District No. 35, school records, 1887-1888. Newton, Kan.: Harvey County Museum and Archives.

While I sat in the Kellas District No. 35 schoolhouse, located on the grounds of the Harvey County Museum and Archives on Main Street in Newton, I looked through the books used for curriculum. I was enamored with the *5th grade Appleton's School Reader* (New York: D. Appleton & Co., 1878), which included poems not only by Shakespeare, but also Lord Byron, Robert Browning, and more. This inspired me to look for suitable poetry with a wintry theme for my book.

O'Gara, *In All Its Fury*, pp. 41, 97-99, 104-105.

William O'Gara's collected firsthand experiences of the Great Blizzard of January 12, 1888. To read some firsthand accounts from Kansas teachers in this book of primarily Nebraska teachers was like finding the proverbial needle in a haystack.

Piersol, M. Interview by the author, November 22, 2019.

Where documentation from books and records seem elusive, a staff voice, Matt Piersol, in the Nebraska State Historical Society edifice of research, resonated with my observation that "schools are numbered in succession of organization within each county."

I encountered such to be the description for South Dakota schools in Turner County (Stoddard, W.H. *Turner County Pioneer History*. Sioux Falls, S.D.: Brown & Saenger, 1931, p. 215).

Ross, D. (1970). *The Illustrated Poetry for Children*. New York: Grosset & Dunlap, 1970, pp. 21, 32.

William Shakespeare (1564-1616) was probably a schoolmaster in his early years. So writing for his pupils doesn't seem to be a stretch of one's imagination. I looked for Shakespeare's biographical information while I searched on Google for the poem, "Blow, Blow, Thou Winter Wind." I discovered lovely renditions of this poem set to music by John Rutter. You can find performances by choirs such as the Cambridge Singers, the Gondwana Singers from New Zealand, and others on YouTube.

Thomas Noel lived 1799-1861. His poem "Old Winter" tells a story and is called a narrative poem.

Smurr, L. (1990). *Harvey County History*. Newton, Kan.: Curtis Media Corporation, 1990, pp. 8-15.

Toevs, D. *Remembering Yesterday, Today*. Kansas Preservation Alliance, 1994, p. 37.

Dudley Toevs' book at the Harvey County Museum and Archives in Newton captures much of Newton's past that helps one remember.

Warkentin House Museum brochure.

Bernhard Warkentin truly helped develop the economy of not only Kansas, but the entire wheat-growing belt with the introduction of Turkey red winter wheat.

Newton (Kan.) Daily Republican, January 12, 1888, p. 1, "Weather."

The Topeka (Kan.) Daily Capital, January 13, 1888, p. 1, "Wichita."

The weather forecast for Kansas in January of 1888 interested me. It came from Washington, D.C., and not from Saint Paul. The commentary on the infamous day, Thursday, January 12, does not include a warning. The weather report the following day indicates nearly four inches of wet snow accumulated in Wichita. By midnight, the thermometer is at 10 degrees above zero.

Chapter Nine: Edith from Enid

Hollon, W. "Oklahoma/Education/Land/Rushes," *World Book Encyclopedia*, Vol.14, 1971, pp. 542, 551, 555-556 a, f, g.

Kraisinger, G. and M. *The Western Cattle Trail* 1874-1897: Its Rise, Collapse, and Revival. Newton, Kan.: Mennonite Press, Inc., 2014, p. 211.

Gary and Margaret Kraisinger are thorough in cattle trail descriptions. Anything one wants to know about cattle trails is well-documented in this jewel of a book.

Our Brother in Red (Muskogee, Indian Territory), January 21, 1888, p. 1, "Blizzard Notes."

Gleaning information of weather from a wider circle during the January 1888 blizzard was a way to double-check information.

Savage, W. *The Cherokee Strip Live Stock Association: Federal Regulation and the Cattleman's Last Frontier.* University of Oklahoma Press, 1990, pp. 1-4.

> I drew upon this article by William Savage for information about the association.

Snodgrass, W. *A History of the Cherokee Outlet.* Dissertation. Oklahoma State University, 1972, p. 11.

> In describing the physical parameters of the Outlet, I relied on information from William George Snodgrass' dissertation.

Wilson, L. "Schools, Subscriptions." *The Encyclopedia of Oklahoma History and Culture, 2020.* www.okhistory.org publications/enc/entry. php?entry=scoo5.

Chapter Ten: Austin from Austin

Frantz, J. "Texas: The Lone Star State." *World Book Encyclopedia*, Vol. 18, 1971, pp. 146-147, 149, 155, 160-163, 166.

> I drew on this resource for information regarding the landscape and culture of Texas.

Globe, January 18, 1888, p. 1. "The Blizzard Victims." *ProQuest Historical Newspapers: The Globe and Mail.*

> This is the first report I found of the Colorado River freezing over since settlement days, so I added the information to the collection of "Weather in Texas and Beyond."

Juhnke and Hunter, *The Missing Peace*, pp. 72, 105-106.

> In thinking of what history might have been or could have been without bloodshed, James Juhnke and Carol Hunter present other options than war that might have been considered or pursued.

O'Gara, *In All Its Fury*, pp. 30-31, 50-51.

> The term "norther," used in the southern states, is described by William O'Gara as a northerly wind with a gale of much force accompanied by a rapidly falling temperature (p. 31).

> My account of weather in Texas and beyond draws on the above pages as noted.

"Protestant Church 1888, Austin, Texas." Wikipedia.

> The article confirms the Protestant presence even though being Catholic was expected of early settlers in Texas.

Epilogue

Much of this book was written during the period of social distancing to limit the spread of the coronavirus pandemic in 2020. I wondered about similarities of social impact this has on the United States in 2020 and the impact the January 12, 1888 blizzard had on the Great Plains and beyond. There is wide disparity in geographical area and population numbers between the Great Plains and the global reaches of this pandemic, yet there are some parallels.

There have been other pandemics, outbreaks, and epidemics – for example, the black plague, Spanish flu, Ebola, and AIDS. So why will we remember COVID-19? The global nature of the virus caught people off guard as it struck without warning. It spread suddenly and rapidly – regardless of age, social status, profession, economic level, or level of intelligence. We all were affected. There is a calm before it actually arrives, thinking we surely will not have the virus here. But the words "suddenly" and "struck without warning" converge into a new reality. Only time will tell what "instructions" will be implemented following this pandemic. Will hospitals now have enough masks and ventilators on hand before the next flu season arrives? Will healthy guidelines for care of the body be taken more seriously?

Just as people during the January 12, 1888 blizzard found ingenious ways to protect themselves and entertain each other, this pandemic has sparked ingenious creativity. People have found amazing ways to connect and celebrate while practicing social distancing. In times of crises we meet life with a spirit in search of normalcy, whether a snowstorm or pandemic.

I admire the fortitude of healthcare workers on the frontline of the pandemic. I also sympathize with those experiencing loss: loss of loved ones to death, loss of a job, loss of a sense of what is normal. Our humanity has been touched in ways that will change the way we relate to others. I hope we will be a kinder and more thoughtful society. I hope we will appreciate "the other" in deeper ways because we have intimately faced mortality. Rediscovering the little things in life is reason for celebration.

Acknowledgments

I am grateful to staff archivists and librarians who helped me locate resources. Thanks to my writer friends, Loretta Baumgartner, Justina Neufeld, and Rachel Poling, who read my manuscript aloud to me. I appreciate my husband, Ron, who faithfully gave his support and was a willing reader. Ron helped identify and explain details that might be unfamiliar to readers. I am grateful to my friend Steven Schurr, a retired meteorologist, who – with good humor – read my unconventional explanations regarding weather. He connected me to helpful websites with historical weather records. Other readers giving observations and editing suggestions were Laurie Oswald Robinson and Melanie Zuercher. My greatest appreciation goes to Timothy L. Waltner. With a keen eye and journalistic bent, he encouraged me to look for consistency and sequence, and to maintain the focus of stories through voice and narrative. His interest in, and grasp of, this writing project kept me grounded. I am grateful to all the readers and their shared wisdom in the process of editing.

Lastly, I'm most grateful to David Laskin for writing *The Children's Blizzard* and to William O'Gara for collecting stories preserved in his book *In All Its Fury: The Great Blizzard of 1888*. I read and reread these books, a real treasure trove. Laskin's and O'Gara's literary contributions provided many details and filled gaps in other resources, enabling me to better weave these stories together.

Cover Design: Lois Thieszen Preheim

More About the Author

Lois and her husband, Ron, volunteered with Mennonite Central Committee for two years in Canada prior to farming for forty-six years near Henderson, Nebraska. Their children are Atlee, Darrin, and Patrick. Over the years, they hosted thirty-seven young adults, ages eighteen through twenty-five, on their farm through the Mennonite Central Committee exchange program. The youth were from eleven different countries. Lois and Ron have visited most of them in their homes; they also enjoy and are privileged to host many of them and their families.

Other oral stories have been preserved, written,
and self-published by Lois Thieszen Preheim:

Apples For Immigrants

Boy Cub:
Rescued by a Lioness

Here We Stand:
Reverend Arnold Nickel
and the Bethesda Mennonite Church
During the Korean War

A Pact: Three Men and a Spade
The beginning of deep well irrigation
for three Henderson, Nebraska farmers 1939-1940

Books are available for purchase;
contact loispreheim@gmail.com for more information.

This photo was taken after reading birthday poems to twin granddaughters, Claire and Tessa, on their seventeenth birthday. Since their birth I have used a different genre of poetry to feature each birthday, encapsulating activities, thoughts, and feelings of the previous year. That prompted me to include poems for each of the chapters in this book.   *Photo Credit: Ron Preheim*